Too soon to say good-bye—
and too late to turn back . . .

Jessica whirled away from the window to face Elizabeth, her blue-green eyes flashing. "Please!" she snarled. "Can we just put a lid on it? First you sneak off to make the most important decision of your life, and then you have the nerve to involve me *now* when it's too late!"

"Jessica!" Elizabeth gasped. "Just wait a minute—"

"No," Jessica interjected angrily. "*You* wait! If you want to go and case out your new joint, be my guest! But remember, just because you have a new life to go to doesn't mean *mine* has to stop!"

"I never said—"

"I've heard *enough*, Elizabeth," Jessica continued, unable to rein herself in. She was on a roll now. "If you want to leave SVU, don't let *me* stop you, but *I* don't have time to talk about it. *I've* got other things to do. Like right now!"

"What do you mean?" Elizabeth exclaimed. "I thought we were going to have lunch together." She gestured at the food lamely.

"Well, I guess that's *another* thing you assumed wrong!" Tossing her hair, Jessica flounced toward the door, shooting a cold glare back at Elizabeth. "You can eat alone. I'm off to find a new roommate!"

Bantam Books in the Sweet Valley University series.
Ask your bookseller for the books you have missed.

And don't miss these Sweet Valley
University Thriller Editions:

Visit the Official Sweet Valley Web Site on the Internet at:

http://www.sweetvalley.com

SWEET VALLEY UNIVERSITY®

Breaking Away

Written by
Laurie John

Created by
FRANCINE PASCAL

BANTAM BOOKS
NEW YORK • TORONTO • LONDON • SYDNEY • AUCKLAND

RL 8, age 14 and up

BREAKING AWAY

A Bantam Book / March 1998

Sweet Valley High® *and Sweet Valley University*®
are registered trademarks of Francine Pascal.
Conceived by Francine Pascal.
Produced by Daniel Weiss Associates, Inc.
33 West 17th Street
New York, NY 10011.

ISBN: 0-553-49221-7

Published simultaneously in the United States and Canada

*Bantam Books are published by Bantam Books, a division of Bantam
Doubleday Dell Publishing Group, Inc. Its trademark, consisting of the
words "Bantam Books" and the portrayal of a rooster, is Registered in
U.S. Patent and Trademark Office and in other countries. Marca
Registrada. Bantam Books, 1540 Broadway, New York, New York 10036.*

PRINTED IN THE UNITED STATES OF AMERICA

OPM   0 9 8 7 6 5 4 3 2 1

To Mary Ann Wolf

Chapter One

"Thank goodness it's Friday!" Jessica Wakefield exclaimed as she opened the door to room 28, Dickenson Hall. "Something smells delicious in here," she observed as she dropped her bag on her messy bed and walked over to where her twin sister, Elizabeth, stood stirring a pot of bubbling sauce on the hot plate in their small kitchenette. "You're making us lunch?"

"A special one," Elizabeth confirmed, smiling and brushing a strand of blond hair from her face. "Angel-hair pasta in a delicate tomato sauce, enhanced by fresh cream, garlic, and a touch of basil. What do you think?" She spooned a little of the thick sauce from the pot and held it up for Jessica to taste.

"Mmm, Liz, this is so good, you could convert a vegetarian!" Jessica exclaimed.

Elizabeth laughed. "Jess, it *is* vegetarian!"

1

"Well, what do you know?" Jessica replied, tossing her hair and heading for the fridge.

Elizabeth continued stirring the sauce while Jessica cracked open a can of diet Coke. The room smelled wonderful, and Jessica felt her stomach rumble with hunger. At the same time she was somewhat suspicious. Why had Elizabeth gone to all the trouble of cooking up a gourmet meal for the two of them when pizza was the norm?

I haven't done Liz any great favors lately, Jessica mused, *and as far as I know I haven't won any awards for academic achievement.* . . .

Crunching a carrot, Jessica eyed Elizabeth and pondered the possible reasons behind the pasta, salad, fresh bread, and cherry cheesecake waiting on the countertop. And then a slow dread tugged at her insides. Maybe it had something to do with the rumor she'd heard yesterday. Could it be true? Was Elizabeth *really* thinking about leaving SVU?

And if she is, then why didn't she consult me first? Jessica thought angrily. *Well, there's only one way to find out.* . . .

"So why all the fancy cooking?" Jessica demanded, trying to keep her voice light, hoping against hope that Elizabeth was simply in a good mood, and there was nothing more to it. "It's a long way from nachos and a side salad. Out with it, Liz. What's up?"

Elizabeth took a deep breath and faced Jessica with a tremulous smile. Then, hesitating, she shrugged and turned back to the stove.

"Elizabeth!" Jessica snapped, folding her arms. "You *know* I hate surprises! Spill!"

"OK, OK." Elizabeth licked her lips nervously and put down the sauce spoon. "I . . . I got an offer from another school, Jess. The Denver Center for Investigative Reporting, in Colorado. And I've accepted."

Jessica's mouth dropped open, and she felt as if she'd been kicked in the stomach. "You *what?*" she cried.

Elizabeth simply averted her eyes and went back to stirring the sauce.

So it's true! Jessica realized. *Of all the rumors I hear, why does* this *one have to be on the money?*

Yesterday afternoon Jessica had heard a few women in her dorm buzzing like mad about Elizabeth leaving SVU to go somewhere with her new boyfriend, Scott Sinclair. Jessica had been worried at first, but the more she'd thought about it, the less she'd felt she could take it seriously. Everyone had their own version of the rumor, each one more outlandish than the next. The only consistent element had been a huge argument between Elizabeth and her ex-boyfriend, Tom Watts, in the cafeteria. And that hardly came as a surprise to Jessica.

Even though they were no longer a couple, Elizabeth was still very emotional about Tom. Jessica figured that if Elizabeth had threatened to leave SVU at all, it was only a ploy to make Tom angry. It was just another round in the Wakefield-Watts battle, nothing more.

Anyway, Elizabeth would *never* do something *that* major without analyzing it for weeks until everyone she knew got sick and tired of the subject.

Maybe I just didn't want to believe it could *be true,* Jessica thought miserably. *Maybe I didn't want to believe that Tom Watts had finally pushed her over the edge.*

"So . . ." Jessica swallowed hard. "You're . . . you're really going to leave SVU? This isn't some kind of dumb joke?"

Elizabeth looked into Jessica's eyes beseechingly. "This is for real, Jess. I'm going."

Despite Elizabeth's apologetic expression, Jessica detected a glimmer of pride in her sister's eyes that angered her even more. *She* wants *to go,* Jessica thought. *She probably can't wait to hotfoot it out of here and go strut her stuff in Denver!*

"You're going," Jessica repeated, her voice brittle and low.

"I'd be a fool to pass this up, Jess," Elizabeth insisted. "It's a great opportunity for me, you know?" Biting her lip, Elizabeth touched Jessica's arm gently, her eyes pleading—even a touch watery.

Jessica felt a bolt of white-hot fury shoot through her. *She wants my approval! She actually expects me to be* happy *for her!*

4

"I know this is a shock," Elizabeth continued. "I mean, we've never been separated like this before. . . . But it won't be so bad, Jess. You'll see. I'll come back and visit, and we'll take ski trips in the Rockies and—"

"Save it!" Jessica cut in. "I *hate* ski outfits!"

Elizabeth raised her eyebrows and smiled tentatively.

She thinks I'm joking! Jessica realized, a flush of anger and hurt creeping up her neck. "I'm not kidding, Elizabeth," she said, her voice cold and even. "If you think I'm leaving Sweet Valley sunshine for Rocky Mountain frostbite, then you don't know me very well."

"Oh," Elizabeth responded, her voice small. She removed her hand from Jessica's arm, a look of pain crossing her face.

Momentarily Jessica felt a pang of guilt. She could see she had wounded Elizabeth. *But it's not as bad as what she's doing to me!* she reasoned.

After an awkward silence Elizabeth turned to Jessica with a begging look. "Jess, please, let's not fight," she began. "This is hard for me too."

"When are you leaving?" Jessica asked brusquely as she walked away to look out the window. *Maybe I can buy some time and convince her to stay,* she thought, her mind starting to tick. *I could convince her that she really doesn't want to leave Sweet Valley, that I can't live without her and she can't live without me. . . .*

5

"Well, I'd be starting next semester," Elizabeth replied. "So I'd have to get going pretty soon. I'll have to register, and then there'll be all sorts of orientation stuff. Plus I'll have to get settled in, get used to Denver, find out where everything is, you know. . . ." She was silent for a moment. "So there really isn't all that much time," she finished.

Time enough. Jessica smiled to herself. *I'll be able to come up with a foolproof, patented Jessica Wakefield plan by then.*

"Actually," Elizabeth continued brightly, "I think I might go out there in a couple of weeks. You know, check out the place, see where I'll be living. We could go together," she added, her voice rising with excitement. "What do you say, Jess? You could come to Colorado with me for a few days! I'm sure Mom and Dad would spring for the ticket. And it would be fun!"

Jessica gritted her teeth. Elizabeth's bubbly voice was irritating her, and she felt about to snap. *Why does she have to rub it in?* she fumed. *As if it's not enough that she drops this bomb on me—now she wants to take me on a tour of her new turf!*

Jessica whirled away from the window to face Elizabeth, her blue-green eyes flashing. "Please!" she snarled. "Can we just put a lid on it? First you sneak off to make the most important decision of your life, and then you have the nerve to involve me *now* when it's too late!"

"Jessica!" Elizabeth gasped. "Just wait a minute—"

"No," Jessica interjected angrily. "*You* wait! If you want to go out and case your new joint, be my guest! But remember, just because you have a new life to go to doesn't mean *mine* has to stop!"

"I never said—"

"I've heard *enough*, Elizabeth," Jessica continued, unable to rein herself in. She was on a roll now. "If you want to leave SVU, don't let *me* stop you, but *I* don't have time to talk about it. *I've* got other things to do. Like right now!"

"What do you mean?" Elizabeth exclaimed. "I thought we were going to have lunch together." She gestured at the food lamely.

"Well, I guess that's *another* thing you assumed wrong!" Tossing her hair, Jessica flounced toward the door, shooting a cold glare back at Elizabeth. "You can eat alone. I'm off to find a new roommate!"

"Jess, please don't leave. You're only making things worse!" Elizabeth cried, her voice sad and defeated.

Good! Jessica thought as the door slammed loudly behind her. *Now we're even. Now you're as miserable as I am!*

Elizabeth flopped onto her bed, tears streaming down her cheeks. *I knew she'd take it hard,* she thought, hiccuping a sob into her pillow. *But not* this *hard.*

It had been difficult enough making the decision to go to Colorado, but Jessica's response had really thrown Elizabeth a curve. *Why can't she be happy for me?* Elizabeth wondered miserably.

She sighed and blew her nose. Only hours earlier butterflies of excitement had fluttered all around her. The Denver Center for Investigative Reporting was quite possibly the most prestigious journalism school in the country, and they had accepted her! It had been a dream come true—until her spat with Jessica.

She wrapped her arms around her favorite pillow for comfort. *Perhaps my decision was selfish,* she mused, recalling Jessica's hurt reactions to her news. *After all, Jessica depends on me! We've been through so much together. Now she must think I'm abandoning her.*

Elizabeth shook her head. "But Jessica's being pretty selfish too," she murmured. "She should be proud of me . . . not tearing down my dreams."

Turning onto her back, she stared at the ceiling, wrestling with the voices battling inside her head. *OK. Maybe I did make a self-centered decision. But we can't keep living together forever, in the same room, in the same city. We have to live our own lives and grow up sometime.* Even though Elizabeth knew she was right, it still didn't help the way she was feeling. She swallowed hard, another wave of tears threatening to engulf her.

Sitting up, Elizabeth pushed a strand of wet hair from her tear-stained cheek and forced herself to calm down. *You've got to start acting mature,* she told herself, *for your own sake and for Jessica's. If you stick to your decision, she'll eventually come around and see that it's the right thing.*

"And if she doesn't . . . then that's just too bad."

Elizabeth hadn't made her decision easily. Part of her had leaped to a yes the minute she had read the letter of acceptance. She'd worked on the high-school paper for years, and she'd put in a lot of time and effort at WSVU, the campus television station, until her ugly breakup with Tom Watts, WSVU's manager, drove her away. Then at the *Sweet Valley Gazette,* Elizabeth had helped crack a major scandal at the Verona Springs Country Club with her reporting partner and new boyfriend, Scott Sinclair. Scott had encouraged her to apply to DCIR. If not for him or for her excellent work on her first *Gazette* story, she might never have been offered the opportunity.

And yet another part of Elizabeth had held back, clinging to Sweet Valley: the place, the people, her family. Sweet Valley was all she had ever known. . . .

But I made my choice, Elizabeth reminded herself, *and I have to stick to my guns.*

Elizabeth pulled herself up off the bed and moved to the telephone. She knew that her parents at least would support her move to Colorado. In fact, they'd be *thrilled* for her. Speaking to them would cheer her up.

But as she lifted the receiver Elizabeth changed

her mind. She wanted to be in a happy mood when she called home; Jessica's outburst had dampened her excitement. *And maybe Jess has already talked to them,* Elizabeth thought, biting her thumbnail anxiously. *She might have convinced them that I'm making a mistake. Maybe they're already on her side!*

Elizabeth felt tears welling up in her eyes once more. Shaking her head, she willed herself not to get into a state again. With a sniff and a brush at her eyes, she picked up the phone and began to dial Scott's number.

Scott picked up on the second ring. "Hello?" his deep voice boomed.

"Scott, it's Elizabeth. Could you meet me in front of the English building at three-thirty?"

"OK. Is everything all right?"

Elizabeth swallowed back tears and tried to make her voice sound normal. "I'm fine. I just need to see you. Can you make it?"

"I'll be there at three-thirty."

Elizabeth put down the receiver, her mood lifting slightly at the thought of seeing Scott. *At least I can count on* his *support,* she mused. *And a little support would be nice for a change!*

"I can't believe she's *deserting* me," Jessica wailed dramatically as she sobbed into the Kleenex handed to her by her best friend, Lila Fowler. Jessica was draped across a couch in Theta house, surrounded by comforting, sympathetic sorority sisters. "I just can't believe it," she repeated. "It's a total disaster."

"Not really, Jess," Lila responded while Isabella Ricci squeezed Jessica's shoulders. "I mean, think about all the arguments you've had."

"Liz is a sweetie, but she's always bossing you around," Denise Waters chimed in.

"You've always had totally opposite takes on everything, Jessica." Lila's perfectly tweezed brows arched in solidarity. "Now you'll be able to express yourself without her disapproving eye on you all the time."

"Easy for you to say," Jessica snapped, grabbing a wad of tissues from the table. "You don't know what it's like to be a twin. Besides, who's going to clean up and keep things organized when Liz goes? She always gets the groceries and sorts through the junk mail. . . ."

"Sounds like Jess is going to have to grow up!" Isabella laughed, and the others smiled in agreement. "Now tell me, Jessica, are you going to miss your sister because she's your sister or your maid?"

Jessica shot Isabella a look of annoyance and continued sniffing into her Kleenex. *Nobody understands,* she thought, her blue-green eyes shining with tears. "This is not a joke, you guys," she announced. "And if you can't see that, then you should probably leave me alone."

"So you can wallow in misery all by yourself?"

11

Lila asked, patting her friend's hand. "That's not like you. Really, Jess, you've *got* to get it together."

"But I don't know how!"

"Look," Isabella added, a smile playing at the corners of her mouth. "You're not seeing this in quite the right way. First of all, think of Liz for a moment."

"Do I have to?" Jessica mumbled crossly. "I can only handle one person's feelings at a time."

"We know, Jessica." Isabella chuckled and twisted a strand of her lustrous, jet-black hair. "But honestly, this really is a good opportunity for her."

"Hmmph."

"OK, then think of *yourself*," Isabella added. She smiled when Jessica perked up with interest. "There we go—*that* seems to be working!"

"Get to the point, Izzy," Jessica snapped.

"OK." Isabella slid onto the couch beside Jessica and grinned, her slate gray eyes twinkling mischievously. "Turn off the tears. This is the best thing that ever happened to you!"

"What are you talking about?" Jessica sniffed and frowned in confusion.

"Now you can get to be the Jessica Wakefield you really are!" Isabella announced. "And you get to be that daring damsel *all the time*, without Elizabeth throwing her two cents in and slamming on the brakes at every turn."

Jessica considered this for a moment. Isabella's words were beginning to make sense. "Well, go on," she demanded impatiently.

"For example. Scenario one: Jessica comes home late from date with Nick and decides to skip class. Outcome: Elizabeth wakes Jessica and scolds her."

"Example two," Lila broke in. "Jessica spots gorgeous outfit in shop window and charges it. Outcome: Elizabeth sees large bill on credit card and reports to Dad."

"Scenario three," Denise offered with a giggle. "Jessica decides to take sorority sisters for moonlight Jeep ride on beach. Outcome: Elizabeth hijacks Jeep to put in quality time at distant library."

"Hmmm . . . I'm beginning to see your point." Jessica sat up and pushed her hair from her face. Her friends made total sense. This *could* be a blessing in disguise.

"Just think of all the fun you're going to have, Jess," Denise said, her big blue eyes wide with awe. "You are about to become queen of spontaneity, wild woman of the West—"

"No holds barred," Lila broke in. "We can shop till we drop, and you can throw the most *extravagant* and *outrageous* parties this side of the Rockies without any wet blanket journalists getting in your way, trying to turn you into a feminist hippie."

"Oh, Lila," Jessica retorted, amused. "Elizabeth isn't *that* bad."

"Well, she certainly doesn't have the best fashion sense," Lila argued, flipping back her glossy brown hair. "There's another thing you won't miss when she's gone—her *clothes!*"

"Fair enough," Jessica admitted. It was true. Of course, the twins were nearly identical in appearance, from their long blond hair and blue-green eyes to their trim, athletic figures. But Jessica and Elizabeth were as different as night and day in virtually every other respect—including their approach to fashion. Spontaneous, thrill-addicted Jessica always embraced every up-to-the-second trend, whereas Elizabeth, ever the serious student, was more interested in the latest dead writer's memoir than the latest concept in shoe design!

Jessica smiled and felt her spirits lighten as her friends continued to dream up scenarios of potential post-Elizabeth fun: middle-of-the-week midnight swimming parties with no Elizabethan lectures on sleep deprivation, all-day tanning sessions at the beach during study week followed by champagne cocktails to toast the sunset . . . and again, no Elizabeth to spoil the fun. The Thetas were right: She and Elizabeth would *thrive* on separation.

Just then, however, a picture of Elizabeth packing up her belongings flashed before Jessica's eyes, and she felt her anger and grief return.

She went behind your back and decided to leave just like that! Jessica reminded herself grimly. *My friends are right—I'd be better off on my own!*

"So when're you going to throw your first party, Jess?" Denise asked brightly.

"Party?" The devious wheels in Jessica's brain began to turn. "That's a great idea, Denise. We should throw a party . . . for my sister."

Isabella's brow wrinkled in thought. "A congratulations party?"

"No," Jessica replied flatly. "A *good-bye* party."

"Oooh, good idea," Lila agreed. "When?"

"As soon as possible." Jessica smiled wickedly. "Then the fun can begin!"

Chapter Two

"... I opened the door to the storage room and hey, presto! Three squirrels jumped out to greet me."

[Cue anchor] "Oakley Hall's head dorm counselor offered no indication as to when the hole in the dormitory's foundation would be fixed...."

Tom Watts yawned and rubbed his eyes, blocking out the sight of the words on his computer screen. Groaning, he glanced at the clock on the desk in front of him. Only one o'clock, and already he felt wiped out from his day at WSVU.

C'mon, Watts, concentrate! he chided himself, willing his eyes back to the story he was working on. "Who cares about some stupid squirrels?" he asked, his voice echoing around the empty office. He longed to forget the story and call it a day, but he knew he couldn't. The squirrel story was the big lead for the Friday night campus news broadcast.

It had been an awfully slow news day.

Maybe I can beef it up a bit, make it more exciting, Tom thought. *Not likely,* he acknowledged ruefully. *Especially since I can't seem to concentrate for more than five seconds.*

But it was just too hard to get focused these days. In the past Tom had always been an enthusiastic reporter, eagerly working into the small hours to get a story tweaked just right. But lately things had been moving steadily downhill, and Tom's thirst for reporting had been replaced by a stronger obsession: the pursuit of Elizabeth Wakefield.

Rocking back on his chair, Tom recalled the early days of his junior year at WSVU, back when he and Elizabeth had been a team. They had had so much energy together and had inspired each other to push for more when it came to their stories.

Tom swallowed painfully as he remembered how passionate he and Elizabeth had once been. *And not just about journalism,* he thought, smiling at the bittersweet memory of the love they had shared—love that had grown and seemed so promising, only to be cut short.

The breakup should never have happened. Everything had been going beautifully until Elizabeth accused Tom's long lost biological father, George Conroy, of making a pass at her. Tom winced at the memory of not believing her.

Well, how could I have? he asked himself. *Who would believe an accusation like that?*

Sighing, Tom rested his chin on his hands and willed himself to focus on the story before him and forget about Elizabeth.

This was becoming a familiar pattern.

You've got to move on, Watts, he scolded himself. *Elizabeth isn't coming back, and you have to pick up the pieces.*

It wasn't as if Tom didn't have anything without Elizabeth. After all, he had Dana Upshaw—she was beautiful and talented, and she adored him completely.

But she's not Liz, he thought mournfully. *No one could ever take her place. She's one of a kind.*

Frustrated to the core, Tom exploded with a curse and slammed his fist onto his desk. His bottle of water teetered but thankfully didn't spill.

"Great! Spill the water, break the computer, and mess up more than just your stupid feelings!" Tom pushed away from his desk and sulked. This endless obsession with Elizabeth was interfering with everything.

What was worse was knowing the feelings weren't mutual. Elizabeth didn't act like she cared about Tom at all—she hadn't even bothered to answer the letter he'd given her, a letter in which he'd swallowed his pride and spilled his guts! No, she was too busy with her new boyfriend, Scott Sinclair, the star journalist.

"What a weasel," Tom muttered as the cocky face of his competitor flooded his vision. Infuriated by an article in the national magazine *NEWS2US* that made Scott come off like the savior of the world press while Elizabeth toiled away as his dizzy, love-struck girlfriend, Tom had discovered that not only was Scott's father connected to the magazine, but he also had ties to the Denver Center of Investigative Reporting—a prestigious journalism school that had recently accepted the happy, loving couple.

But even after Tom had broken the news on WSVU, Elizabeth still hadn't seen fit to kiss that loser good-bye. In fact, she'd lashed out at Tom yesterday in the student union cafeteria, accusing *him* of trying to hurt *her* with his report.

"Has Elizabeth gone deliberately blind?" Tom muttered in frustration. But the more he thought about it, the more he began to believe otherwise. *Maybe she got upset because she still cares about me a little,* he mused. *Maybe she just needs more time to sort things out.*

Just then the piercing shrill of the station phone broke into Tom's thoughts. For a second his heart leaped wildly. Maybe it was Elizabeth! *Maybe right now we're having some kind of telepathic connection,* he imagined. *She's thinking about me too and wants to clear the air once and for all.*

But before he even picked up the phone, Tom's hopes took a dive. If there was one thing

Elizabeth was, it was proud. Reluctantly Tom had to admit that the probability of a reconciliation right now, especially after their last angry show-down, was extremely low.

"Hey, Tom." The unmistakable deep voice belonging to Danny Wyatt, Tom's best friend and roommate, filled his ear when he picked up the phone. Tom heaved a sigh of disappointment. Despite his own reasoning, he always had hope for a miracle. But miracles and Elizabeth Wakefield didn't seem to go together very well.

"What's up?" Tom inquired disinterestedly, deleting the one and only line he'd written in the last hour from the computer screen.

"Just checking in."

"Sorry . . . I'm kind of busy," Tom replied. "No time to shoot the breeze, pal." He wasn't in the mood for idle conversation, even with Danny. Or maybe *especially* with Danny, whose sickly sweet relationship with gorgeous Isabella Ricci only rubbed salt into Tom's wounds these days.

"I've got an interesting piece of news, though," Danny offered.

"Will it help with my story?" Tom asked. "You know this squirrels in Oakley Hall piece could use a kick."

"Can't help you there, Tombo." Danny chuckled. "Hey, why don't you just spice it up a little with some fiction? Say they aren't just ordinary

21

squirrels but instead are rumored to belong to a rare killer breed."

"Please!" Tom laughed. "Killer squirrels on the loose at SVU! Just as well you aren't a journalist, Danny. You know, we can't just suck things out of thin air, contrary to popular belief. There has to be a nugget of truth in every story."

"That reminds me. I've got a nugget for you from a story I heard today."

"And what's that?" Tom grabbed the bottle of water beside him and drained it. He felt tired again. *Tired and bored*, he thought glumly.

"It's about Elizabeth."

"Oh?" Instantly Tom felt wide awake. He sat up in his chair.

"She's leaving SVU," Danny continued.

Tom felt as if he had been slugged in the chest; for a moment he couldn't breathe. "Wha-What are you talking about?" he stammered.

"Remember that fight you guys had in the cafeteria yesterday? When you told her to go to Denver with Scott if she thought he was so great?"

Dread chilled Tom to his very soul. "Yes," he replied weakly.

"Well, she is."

"She is?" Tom repeated. His mouth went dry, and he closed his eyes.

"She's been accepted to DCIR and she's going, Tom."

"Are you serious?"

"I'm serious," Danny reiterated, the words descending on Tom's ears like blows to the head. "I heard about an hour ago. Everyone's talking about it."

Tom felt his heartbeat begin to accelerate, and he shook his head, gripping the phone receiver tighter in his sweaty hand. He refused to accept Danny's words. Maybe there was some mistake. A misinterpretation, an error in communication. These things happened all the time, especially when it came to Elizabeth.

And yet maybe it *was* true. It would serve Tom right for making that comment about following Scott to Denver. *But I never believed she would take me seriously!* Tom thought in desperation. *I thought she was just trying to bait me. Not for a second did I think she'd really leave Sweet Valley!* After another stunned silence he finally managed to speak again. "When did she tell you?"

"She didn't," Danny replied.

"Well, then, who did?" Tom demanded impatiently. Sometimes getting information from Danny was like drawing blood from a stone.

"Isabella told me."

Tom's mouth dropped open in shock. Isabella! Then slowly a smile spread across his face and he rolled his eyes, heaving a sigh of relief. Isabella was a typical Theta, always gossiping, always "hearing" stories three times removed. This was something he and Elizabeth used to laugh about. Women like

Isabella, Jessica, and Lila were typically so busy "keeping their ears flapping" as Elizabeth called it that they probably wouldn't know a real piece of news from a rumor if they saw it happen right in front of their noses.

Tom laughed, a mixture of annoyance and relief churning inside him. "Now *that's* the gospel truth," he added sarcastically. "Danny, don't take this the wrong way, but in the reporting world your girlfriend is what is known as 'an unreliable source.'"

"I suppose you think Isabella can't tell fact from fiction," Danny responded coolly.

"That's exactly what I'm saying," Tom replied. "Come on, you know how those Thetas are. How many of their press-stopping news items have turned out to be true? They spend their lives gossiping, Danny."

"Yeah, I know," Danny admitted. "But just because Isabella heard it doesn't make it fiction either."

As much as Tom hated to admit it, Danny was right. The story *might* have some truth to it. The odds were slim, but still, Tom couldn't pretend that the conversation he'd had with Elizabeth didn't exist.

Tom raked his hands through his hair nervously. Beads of perspiration dotted his forehead. He needed some air, some time to think things through on his own. "Listen, Danny, I really have to get back to work. I'll catch you later, OK?"

After Danny hung up, Tom sat for a moment cradling the phone receiver in his hand. "It can't be true," he murmured, as if saying it out loud might give his words more power.

Yes, it can, a voice inside him replied.

Tom got up and moved to the window. He opened it and leaned out into the fresh, cleansing air. *Elizabeth wouldn't make such a rash decision,* he told himself. *She wouldn't just pack up and leave her whole life behind.* She had such a full life in Sweet Valley. Her friends, her family, her twin sister, everything she'd ever known was here. *She wouldn't leave all that, would she?*

"She wouldn't . . . she wouldn't leave me," Tom whispered feebly.

Admit it, the voice inside him responded. *She's deciding to leave* because *of you.*

At that, Tom felt his heart begin to pound furiously. It was as if his body were beating the awful truth right through him. *She's gone already,* he told himself miserably. *Might as well face it.*

He turned to stare unhappily around the room. His eyes focused on the old couch where he and Elizabeth used to kiss. Those moments seemed to belong to another lifetime.

A lump as hard as a bird's egg rose in Tom's throat, and he blinked back tears. "It's over," he whispered to the empty room. "It really is over."

*   *   *

Elizabeth glanced around her at the lush trees shading the campus walkway. With their fresh, green leaves and pale peach blossoms, they made every day at SVU feel like the first day of spring. *It certainly is a beautiful campus,* she found herself thinking, the beauty around her a bittersweet reminder of what she would be leaving behind.

Sighing, Elizabeth tried to focus on something besides her move. All the thinking had worn her out, and she needed to get her mind off the heavy stuff for a while. Just then, a few feet ahead of her, she spotted the wild, curly brown hair, ungainly walk, and bizarre clothing combinations that made Winston Egbert hard to miss. Today he was wearing red-checkered golf pants, a bright yellow T-shirt, and an orange vintage vest. She could already feel herself smiling at the sight of her old friend. If anyone could cheer her up, he could.

"Hey, Winston, wait up," Elizabeth called out. "Are you on your way to English lit too?"

"Sure am, Liz," Winston replied, holding up a copy of Virginia Woolf's *Orlando.* "Hey, have you read this? I haven't started yet, but I figure a book about Disney World can't be that bad."

"Oh, Winnie." Elizabeth giggled, her mood lifting. "It's not about Orlando, *Florida,* silly!"

"I know, I know." Winston laughed. "Just pulling your leg. Of course I've read it. Just because you're running around winning scholarships doesn't mean you're the only one who reads, you know! Hey, by the way, Liz, congratulations. It is true, isn't it? You're leaving us?"

"Uh, yeah," Elizabeth replied, her smile growing more forced by the second. "How did you know?"

"Oh, you know this place. You can't breathe without everyone hearing about it."

Elizabeth sighed. It was true. By now the whole campus probably knew she was leaving, which wasn't exactly what Elizabeth wanted. She would have liked to keep her decision under wraps for a little while, at least until she had completely gotten used to the idea herself.

"Liz!"

Elizabeth looked up to see Isabella Ricci, looking fresh and pretty in a short red gingham dress. "Jessica told me your news!" she enthused. "Way to go!"

Jessica—of course! Elizabeth realized as she thanked Isabella. *The whole world must know by now. Never mind the information superhighway—Jessica Wakefield can spread news faster than anything or anyone!*

"Hey, if it isn't Sweet Valley's own star journalist!" Bruce Patman called out. He stopped Elizabeth at the foot of the stairs to the lit lecture room and threw his arms around her. "Not bad, Liz. Not bad!"

Elizabeth thanked Bruce and excused herself, leaving Bruce and Winston chatting behind her.

27

She took a deep breath at the top of the stairs. *News sure travels fast,* she thought, smiling ruefully. Glancing at the door to the lecture room, she paused before entering and considered sitting out in the corridor until everyone was seated inside. Another round of congratulations was certain to await her; while she found it touching, Elizabeth knew she couldn't handle it quite yet. After a moment she took a deep breath. *Might as well face the music,* she told herself, heading for the door. But someone had beaten her to it.

What's Tom *doing here?* she wondered, her nerves jangling. *He's not in this class.* And then it dawned on her. *He still remembers my schedule,* she realized, lowering her eyes. *He must be here to talk to me!*

Elizabeth felt her stomach give a little flip. Perhaps Tom was there to congratulate her . . . or maybe beg her not to go. *Not likely,* she acknowledged unhappily. Their last few meetings had been colored by angry words and insults. There was no reason this one should be any different.

Elizabeth swallowed hard and looked up at Tom. A cold feeling of dread spread through her insides, and she walked toward him woodenly, mentally trying to prepare herself for whatever harsh words were about to come her way.

Tom's expression was as hard and cold as marble, and Elizabeth felt as if her knees were about to cave in. *Why does he still have the power to upset me like this?* she wondered angrily. Would Tom Watts and his opinions of her ever *not* matter in her life?

"Hello, Elizabeth." Tom's voice was brittle, and he folded his arms defensively.

"Hello," Elizabeth replied coolly, chiding herself for having had such foolish hopes earlier. *As if he would come to congratulate me. There's more chance of a Martian landing on the football field than that!*

Miserably she wondered why she continued to have such irrational hopes when it came to Tom. He had proved over and over again that any dreams of reconciliation Elizabeth might have had were completely unfounded. So why did she continue to be disappointed and hurt by him?

It's called living in a fool's paradise, she berated herself. *And now it's time to get real.*

Hardening her heart, Elizabeth turned to face him, her jaw set rigidly. "Why are you here, Tom?" she asked, her voice even and controlled.

Tom seemed taken aback by Elizabeth's frigid reception, and Elizabeth felt a little bolt of satisfaction shoot through her. *Serves him right!* She glared at him, willing herself to maintain a calm and distant composure.

But it was hard not to give slightly at the sight of him. *Although he doesn't look too good today,* she observed. Tom was usually very well-groomed, but his face was gaunt, his eyes were red, and he looked disheveled.

"Well." Tom cleared his throat and took a step back toward the door of the lecture hall. "I wasn't aware that I had to have *your* permission to stand here," he continued, his voice cutting.

Elizabeth was taken aback. Why did he have to be *so* unbelievably mean to her all the time? Wasn't it enough that he had hurt her deeply? Did he have to keep chopping her up into little pieces too?

"Fine, Tom," she spat, shaking with anger. "Go ahead, stand wherever you want. But in the future don't greet me when you see me! I don't need these special little moments in my day, OK?"

Armed with an angry fake smile, she attempted to push past Tom, but he blocked her path.

"Before you go, Elizabeth," he began, his voice dripping with venom, "I have something to say to you."

Elizabeth stood silently, her face burning.

"I want you to know that I think you made the right decision," Tom continued, his voice rising with emotion. "I'm glad you're leaving, Elizabeth. I'm really, *really* glad."

Raising her eyebrows, she managed a tentative thank-you. She couldn't even guess what Tom was thinking right now.

He nodded in response. "You see, this works out best for both of us," Tom continued. "Because I never, *ever* want to see you again!"

Elizabeth's hand flew to her chest and she gasped, but Tom had already turned his back on her and was storming away down the corridor.

"And by the way," he shouted over his shoulder. *"Congratulations!"*

Tears began to sting her eyelids, and Elizabeth felt them spill over onto her cheeks. But she made no attempt to brush them away. *It doesn't matter,* she thought bitterly as she felt her classmates' eyes on her. *Nothing matters, because no one cares! Not Jessica, not Tom . . . only Scott.*

I guess Tom is right, she told herself as hot tears coursed down her neck and into her shirt collar. *I did make the right decision. It's time for me to kiss the past good-bye and get on with my life.*

Dana Upshaw sipped her cappuccino and wrinkled her small, delicate nose. Campus coffee was the worst! She frowned, tossing back her long mane of curly mahogany hair, and looked at her schedule for the next week. A Spanish quiz, two papers due, and four cello lessons to give—that left practically no spare time to spend with Tom.

Still, Dana had reason to be in a good mood. A sly smile crept across her face as she remembered the great news she'd heard. Elizabeth Wakefield, the ice queen, would be leaving Sweet Valley!

Out of my hair once and for all, Dana thought with a silent cheer. Finally she would have Tom all to herself with no threat of any further trouble on that chilly front.

Tom had really been driving Dana crazy lately.

31

Despite the fact that she gave him everything he could ever need, he hadn't seemed to dispose of his feelings for his frostbitten ex.

For a moment Dana cast her mind back to all the times Tom had been moody or preoccupied—all thanks to Elizabeth, of course. She'd had to work *so* hard to keep them apart, right down to intercepting a treacly love letter Tom had written to her.

Well, luckily she never got it, Dana mused. *And now she'll never get him either!* Dana smiled with satisfaction at the thought of Elizabeth's departure. *As soon as that plane takes off with Elizabeth on it, I can relax. Until then I just have to sit tight.*

"Hey, is this seat open?"

Dana came out of her reverie to see who was speaking to her. "I guess," she replied, looking up to see the chiseled face of Scott Sinclair, the ice queen's latest pawn. Dana frowned. *Why does he want to sit with me?* she wondered. *We don't exactly know each other, and there are plenty of empty seats around.*

"So . . . ," Scott began. "How's life?"

"Uh, *fine*," Dana replied, giving him a quizzical look. "Same old, same old."

"Yup," Scott offered, and then fell silent. He didn't seem to know what else to say, and yet he remained in his seat, staring at Dana. She shifted in discomfort.

"So . . . how are you?" Dana ventured in an attempt to break the silence.

"Good. Really good. Been spending a lot of time with Elizabeth Wakefield."

What does he want, a medal? Dana wondered, completely clueless as to why Scott was bringing this up. *So he's with Elizabeth. Great! It keeps the snob out of my way at least, but talking about her is a* major *waste of my time!*

"I hear she's off to Colorado," Dana said. *Guess I'm going to have to make small talk until he goes away,* she thought, irritated at the prospect of a boring conversation with someone she barely knew and didn't much care for.

"Really?" Scott answered, a look of surprise on his face. "Wow, I had no idea she'd made a decision."

Dana studied Scott's expression. What was going on? He looked and acted surprised at the news, but Dana could tell by the way his eyes skittered nervously that he was just putting on an act. *I can spot a liar a mile away,* she thought, *and this guy needs some lessons in deception. He should hang around me more often,* she added silently, half amused and half ashamed at her own shrewd self-analysis.

But why was he lying? And why was he sitting at Dana's table? Dana gave Scott a searching look, which he didn't seem to notice. Or was choosing to ignore. *Fine,* Dana thought, folding her arms, *keep me in suspense if you want. Let's see what games you can play . . . and if you can keep up with* me!

"So how are things with you and Tom?" Scott asked with a tentative smile.

Dana's jaw practically fell to the floor. This was so completely out of her orbit! Why did he care? Did he want to ask her out? Surely not! He was dating Elizabeth, wasn't he?

Not that that stopped anybody where you're concerned, a voice whispered inside her, and Dana felt her face go red with hurt and frustration at the thought of Tom and his seemingly undying devotion to Her Royal Highness, the reigning queen of Iceland. Swallowing hard, Dana fought to regain her composure. She couldn't let anyone even remotely connected with Elizabeth think that she and Tom were anything less than airtight. "Things couldn't be better between me and Tom," she answered, her voice even.

"So you guys . . . you're happy together?"

"Yes," Dana said, her voice betraying the impatience she felt. *What is up with this guy?* she wondered. *He's a bit on the slow side—the light's on, but there's no one home! Or maybe he's the paranoid, jealous type who thinks Tom's going to kidnap his precious Elizabeth and take her off to some isolated cabin in the woods. . . .*

"That's good." Scott smiled, his teeth toothpolish bright. "I'm very glad to hear that." Slowly he stood up and ran a hand through his thick blond hair. Looking at Dana again, he flashed her a grin. "Keep it that way," he added softly. He winked at her conspiratorially and picked up his backpack. Without a backward glance he left the cafeteria.

Dana's mouth dropped open. *What was that all about?* she wondered. What could Scott have meant by that cryptic comment? Completely bewildered, Dana shook her head and then picked up the cello propped on the floor beside her. She had to get moving. She had a kid to teach, and she was late. *And all because of that weirdo,* she thought as she maneuvered past a couple of students.

On her way out the door Dana recalled the way Scott had winked at her before he left. *As if we're in on some secret,* she reflected. *Or like we've made some kind of deal.* As she moved down the passage Dana replayed the peculiar exchange in her mind, but she couldn't put her finger on what had really taken place. *Well, I guess I'll find out soon enough. All good things come to those who wait!*

Chapter
Three

_____

"Winston! Aren't you supposed to be in class?"
Denise exclaimed, widening her big blue eyes as
Winston plopped himself beside her on the stairs
outside Oakley Hall.

"Missed you too much," Winston replied, tilting
Denise's chin for a kiss. "And that lit class was so
boring, I fell asleep twice before I managed to slip
out the door. Honestly, that Professor Cartright is a
mummy. He could use some CPR, pronto."

Denise raised an eyebrow in confusion.

"Someone needs to breathe some life into
him," Winston explained. "'We nohhhte that the
chaaaracters in this tehhhxt,'" he mimicked, "'de-
vehhhlop the themaaatic cohhhntent in that . . .'"

Denise laughed and shook her head at her
boyfriend, her neat chestnut bob swinging as she
moved. "Oh, Winnie." She sighed, resting her
head on his arm. "Even when I'm not in the

mood for laughing, you always manage to crack me up."

"It's what I'm here for, madam," Winston replied, pulling his mouth into a grimace and screwing up his eyes. "It's my mission in this lifetime, and one that I take most seriously."

"Speaking of serious," Denise began, her voice clouding over with anxiety, "I've been sitting out here for ages, dreading going inside. Judging by the calls I've been receiving lately, the credit card companies are beginning to take me very seriously indeed."

"You in some kind of fiduciary trouble?" Winston asked in a Mickey Mouse voice.

"Winston!" Denise frowned. "Stop kidding around. Not everything's a joke, you know!" Her lip began to tremble, and she ran a hand through her hair worriedly. What had started out so innocently had turned into nothing short of a nightmare!

It all began when Denise discovered that a small plastic rectangle could change her life significantly. She hadn't meant to get into such debt, but it had crept up on her silently and sneakily. By the time she realized the extent of the damage she had done, it was too late. She was in a financial pit, and it was going to take some major ingenuity to dig herself out.

Groaning, Denise mentally reviewed the expensive dinners she'd bought, the gifts for Winston, and her new wardrobe. It had all been so easy and too tempting to resist, especially since everyone else at SVU appeared to have no problem spending money like water. And Denise had wanted a taste of that freedom desperately. She longed to pick and choose from mail-order catalogs and designer shoe stores like Lila and Isabella did every day.

But it was only meant to be a taste *of luxury, Denise,* she chided herself. *You were only supposed to have a spoonful of the dessert, not eat the whole bowl!*

And yet once she'd started, she couldn't stop. Money—or its plastic substitute anyway—was an intoxicating thing, and Denise had allowed herself to be lured by its charms. She'd overspent on one card, which caused a chain reaction leading to a lock on her financial aid and student loans. Her college career in jeopardy, she'd contacted another bank, which had promised to consolidate her debts and send some cash her way. But she'd already spent the cash that was supposed to be applied to her first payment, and the credit line they'd extended her didn't even come close to consolidating her debt. Now she was chin deep in red tape, and everyone and their dog was asking her for payment. The whole thing made Denise's head spin and her eyes water.

"Sorry, Denise," Winston began, gently breaking her train of thought. "I was just trying to cheer you up. I know this stuff is really upsetting you."

"That's OK, Winnie." Denise tried to smile but only managed a small twist of her mouth. "It's not your fault that I'm in this mess. I've only got myself to blame for being so stupid. And maybe I *could* use a little lightening up."

"Don't call yourself stupid, stupid," Winston replied, chucking her gently under the chin. "I happen to think you're the rain in Spain . . . the belle of the ball . . . the queen of them all!"

Denise laughed and ruffled her hand through Winston's wild mop of hair. *At least I have a wonderful boyfriend,* she thought. *Although it won't matter much when I'm behind bars.* With a gloomy sigh she stood up. It was time to face her answering machine. She couldn't put it off forever.

"Come on, let's go inside," she said, grabbing Winston's arm and helping him to his feet. "I'm going to have to sooner or later, and I think I'd rather face this with you."

"Worry not, fair lady," Winston declared. "For you are with me, and I will be your rock." He flexed his biceps playfully. "I shall shoulder your burdens, protect you from the storm."

Denise rolled her eyes and giggled at Winston's ridiculous bodybuilder pose. With his stringy, golf-ball-size biceps, Winston wouldn't be winning any jock contests anytime soon.

"I am your warrior," Winston continued. "Your own personal gladiator."

"Winston Egbert, do you *ever* shut your trap?" Denise asked.

"Not if I can help it. It is the portal of wisdom, the conduit of sage truths and witty epiphanies—"

"And also the source of complete nonsense," Denise added. "If you don't watch out, your portal might get closed down," she warned jokingly. "In the middle of the night I'll sneak into your room and Scotch tape that mouth of yours. Then perhaps we'll have some peace and quiet in the world, if only for a moment."

Winston acted shocked and pretended to choke Denise as they made their way up the stairs. "Silence, woman!" he declared, his voice boomingly theatrical. "Lest you may find yourself in a dark place!"

Denise smiled ruefully at Winston's words. *A dark place,* she thought. *Like in a debtors' prison cell!*

"Liz, over here!"

Scott waved from a booth in the SVU cafeteria and Elizabeth made her way over to him, grateful to see his friendly smile. It had been a horrible afternoon. Elizabeth had barely heard a word of the Virginia Woolf lecture. All she'd heard were the angry voices of Tom and Jessica going through her mind, together with her own inner voice wondering if her life-altering decision had been a foolish one.

The clanging in her head had been so unbearable

41

that she'd had to leave class five times to cry in the bathroom. Now she had a pounding headache, and her eyes were red and swollen. *It'll be OK*, she told herself. *You've just had an emotional day, and you've been under too much pressure. It's natural to break down once in a while!*

But deep down, Elizabeth wondered if it was more than just the pressures involved with her decision that had made her cry. The nasty exchange with Tom in front of the lit room had really thrown her off-balance. Just seeing Tom's face had opened old wounds *and* brought back memories of happier times. And it wasn't just this time but *every* time she saw Tom that he had that effect on her.

You're not ready to say good-bye, Elizabeth's inner voice whispered. Instantly she forced that notion from her mind, denying it vehemently. *I don't care about leaving Tom*, she told herself. *In fact, I'm looking forward to it!*

"Uh, Earth to Elizabeth!"

"Huh?" Elizabeth looked up from the floor, momentarily disoriented.

"You look as if you've left the planet," Scott added.

"Oh, sorry," Elizabeth mumbled as she slid into a seat. "I've had a long day. I guess I'm kind of in a daze."

"You're forgiven," Scott replied, touching Elizabeth's shoulder affectionately.

Elizabeth smiled gratefully in return. *Scott really is a sweet guy,* she found herself thinking. *He's always concerned with my well-being—unlike* some *people I know.*

She pushed that thought from her mind as fast as it had arrived. She'd vowed to stop fixating on Tom and to focus instead on those few people she knew who genuinely cared for her. People like Scott.

"So, Liz, what can I get you? Coffee? Champagne?"

"I've got my water, thanks," Elizabeth replied, bursting into laughter as she finally digested Scott's words. "Champagne?" she repeated, bemused.

"Well, I'd get champagne for you if they served it," Scott replied, taking her hand in his. "I heard the news this morning. It's fantastic, Liz. Congratulations!"

With that, Scott stood and pulled Elizabeth up with him into a big hug. "I'm so proud of you," he murmured, kissing the top of her head. "You're incredible!" He lifted her up until her feet left the ground and squeezed her tightly.

Laughing, Elizabeth demanded to be put down. "I don't want to make a scene," she said. "It seems to be all I do lately." But Scott's enthusiasm and spontaneous affection touched her so much, she felt a warm tingling glow of pleasure spread through her. If only everyone felt that way about her decision!

As they settled back into the booth Scott's eyes found Elizabeth's and he grinned at her, covering her hands with both of his. "This is just the beginning," he declared, his piercing blue eyes shining. "Great things lie ahead for us."

"I sure hope so," Elizabeth said as Scott brought her hands to his lips and kissed them. "And if it weren't for you, I wouldn't be going."

At first Elizabeth had been reluctant to get involved with Scott. He'd seemed a little too pushy for her, too smothering. But she came to realize that she'd only been resisting him because the wounds from her breakup with Tom hadn't yet healed. Slowly but surely she'd begun to be won over by his charm, his intelligence, and his attentiveness to her needs.

He's been so good to me, she reflected, studying the handsome face before her. Scott's clear, crystalline blue eyes, chin-length, sun-streaked blond hair, and strong jaw made him a real find—a diamond sparkling among dull, lifeless rhinestones. *But most important,* Elizabeth concluded, *he's a kind, decent person. His looks don't even begin to measure up to the heart beating inside him.*

She squeezed Scott's hands proudly. *I'm so lucky to have found him,* she mused. *He was willing to give me the space I needed to get over Tom and move on. He's taught me that it's OK to give new things a chance.*

"It's time for a change," Scott said.

"That's just what I was thinking," Elizabeth replied, amazed. "Although all day I've been wondering if I made the right decision."

"You did." Scott traced Elizabeth's cheek with a finger. "I know this is going to work out." His eyes sparkling, he leaned over and kissed Elizabeth tenderly.

His lips were so gentle that Elizabeth relaxed and allowed herself to enjoy the softness of Scott's kiss. As his lips covered hers again, she found her spirits lifting and began to kiss him back. When they finally broke apart, Elizabeth sighed happily and looked up at Scott with warmth. She felt safe and reassured by the loving look in Scott's eyes. He was right. Everything *would* work out.

"Here's to our future!" Scott held up his coffee cup and touched it to Elizabeth's bottle of water.

"To our future," Elizabeth repeated, leaning over to kiss Scott again. As her lips found his she closed her eyes. *Finally,* she thought. *I'm finally moving on with my life!*

"OK, here goes!" Denise took a deep breath and turned the key in her mailbox.

Winston squeezed her hand as she withdrew a stack of mail. "Don't worry," he said comfortingly. "It'll be OK."

They walked up the stairs to Denise's room, and she opened the door with trembling hands. "I can't help it, Winnie." She sighed. "I'm terrified.

It's got so that I can't even bear to come home. I'm afraid of the mail and afraid of the phone." She glanced over at her answering machine. "Great," she murmured. "It's lit up like a Christmas tree!"

"That could be a good sign," Winston ventured. "Look on the bright side. Maybe it's full of messages inviting us to parties . . . or maybe it's someone calling to tell you you've won the lottery."

"That's what I need." Denise sighed longingly. "To win the lottery! Then all our troubles would be over, and we could retire in style before we've even entered the job market."

"Wouldn't *that* be something," Winston replied dreamily. "I see myself on a yacht, sailing around the Greek isles. Me—bronzed and handsome at the helm of a sleek, elegant twenty-foot yacht, you—tanning on the deck, wearing big Jackie O. sunglasses!" Winston's eyes had a faraway look in them as he stared out the window, caught up in his fantasy.

"Dream on, sailor," Denise quipped, opening an official-looking envelope. "It's not happening."

Her heart quickened as she began to scan the notice in her hand. *You have exceeded your cash limit for the month of May,* the text read in thick, black letters.

"Oh, boy," Denise murmured. "In the red again!"

"What does it say?" Winston asked, grabbing

the letter from her hands. He frowned as he read the ominous words. "Denise, this *is* pretty bad," he admitted. "It says here that this is your second credit offense—and that you can't use cash advances to pay your minimum."

"I know," Denise wailed, sinking onto her bed. "It's a total disaster. If I can't use cash advances, then I can't pay the minimum. And I can't pay the minimum because I'm *still* trying to pay off my other bills. It's a vicious cycle! I'm like a dog chasing its tail!"

"Now look," Winston began, his voice calm and matter-of-fact. "Things are bad, but they're not completely hopeless. They have to send you these letters, but they're not *really* going to send the collection agents after you. I mean, you're not some kind of criminal, and they have plenty of bigger fish to chase after. They're not really interested in small fry like you."

"If only that were true," Denise said miserably, staring at the ceiling. "They're already after me. A collection agent has been leaving messages on my machine. It's pretty scary."

"Well, let's see." Winston moved briskly to the answering machine and pushed the play button. The first three messages were from friends, and Denise brightened. Maybe things weren't so bad after all.

"You see?" Winston smiled. "They've given up on you already." But no sooner had he said that than an impersonal female voice filled the air.

"Ms. Waters," the stern, unforgiving voice intoned. *"This is the California Commission for Student Assistance. Please call Ms. Arlene in the collections department immediately at . . ."*

"Oh no!" Denise groaned, burying her face in her pillow.

The next two messages were from the same person, presumably "Ms. Arlene," and her voice grew progressively meaner and more clipped. Finally the machine clicked off and Winston exhaled, a crease of worry forming on his brow.

Denise began to cry, her shoulders heaving and her tears dotting her pillowcase. "Don't you see?" she moaned. "They *are* after me! Oh, Winnie, what am I going to do?"

Winston sat on the bed beside her and stroked her hair. "We'll think of something," he soothed. "I can try and help too. I'll give you my allowance for the month, and we'll just not go out for a while. That's a start."

"Oh, stop." Denise gulped. "That is *so* sweet of you. But I'm afraid your allowance is just a drop in the ocean of my debt."

"I could hock my valuables!" Winston suggested.

Denise sat up and laughed, wiping the tears from her eyes. "Winston, you don't *have* any valuables!"

"I have you," Winston offered, grinning, and

Denise felt a warm ripple of affection melt through her tears. "But," Winston added jokingly, "I guess I can't very well hock you!"

"I guess not," Denise replied, smiling weakly through her tears. She hugged Winston, burying her head in his neck. "But I'm touched—I *think*— that you would sell me to save me," she added, laughing. "No, we'll have to think of something else," she murmured as he stroked her hair. *And I will,* she vowed. *I'm going to come up with a plan, and it's going to be a good one. . . .*

"Liz?" Jessica called out guiltily as she opened the door of their dorm room. She had been feeling bad ever since she'd flounced out of their room that morning. Jessica was still angry with Elizabeth, but she couldn't help the twinges of guilt she'd been feeling all day.

Despite feeling this way, a bubble of annoyance rose up inside her. *I always let Elizabeth get to me,* Jessica thought as her sister looked up at her from where she sat talking on the phone.

"She's here now," Elizabeth said into the receiver. "OK . . . here she is."

Jessica's heart leaped, and for a moment she forgot all about Elizabeth. Nick! She was just in time for his phone call! *I wonder what he has planned for our date tonight,* she thought with excitement. Nick always had something extra-special planned for Friday nights. Jessica grabbed the phone from Elizabeth and turned her back for privacy. "Hi, sweetie," she purred demurely.

"Hi, sweetie, *yourself*," two voices answered back in unison.

Jessica's face lit up like a torch, and she cringed. "Oh . . . uh, hi, Mom! Hi, Dad!" she replied, shocked.

"Expecting someone else?" Mr. Wakefield queried, chuckling.

"Um . . ." Jessica gulped as she trailed off. "What's up?" she continued briskly, eager to change the subject.

"Things are fine with us," Mrs. Wakefield replied. "And we're thrilled to hear Elizabeth's exciting news."

"You are?" Jessica frowned. She'd hoped her parents would feel the same way she did about Elizabeth's leaving Sweet Valley. Without their parents' complete approval, Jessica knew Elizabeth wouldn't go to Colorado.

There's another difference between us, Jessica observed. *Liz always does what they want, and I always want what they forbid!* Sadly, this time their parents appeared to be behind Elizabeth one hundred percent. "Thrilled," Mrs. Wakefield had said. Jessica was crestfallen. No allies in the family on this one!

"How do you feel about this, Jessica?" Mr. Wakefield asked.

Jessica stole a glance at Elizabeth, who smiled back uncertainly. *She really wants my approval,*

Jessica thought, and for a moment she forgot her disappointment and was pleased that her opinion mattered so much. Clearly her parents wanted Jessica's blessing, as did Elizabeth, and between Elizabeth's nervous glances and her parents' concerned voices, Jessica felt rather powerful.

"Well," Jessica began slowly, stalling for time as she considered her options. *I could be generous and selfless,* she reflected, *or I could say what I feel.* After a mere second of deliberation Jessica decided to go with the truth. *I'm a passionate person,* she justified to herself, *and although I know I'll freak everyone out, I can't lie. I'm not the type!*

"I think it's *terrible!*" Jessica exclaimed. "I mean, I know this is a good opportunity for Elizabeth and everything," she continued smoothly, knowing this line of reasoning would appeal to her parents. "But I *can't believe* that she would even *consider* going away from Sweet Valley . . . and all of us!" Jessica ignored the panicked look she was getting from Elizabeth and concentrated on the soothing murmurs of her parents instead. This was good! An impassioned plea could make her parents change their minds. *They might even forbid her to go!* Jessica thought happily, her mind buzzing.

"You know," she continued, infusing her voice with just the right amount of wistful sadness together with a certain worldly air, "there's a saying: He who leaves his castle, leaves his garden. Wait,

51

no!" She screwed up her face in confusion. "That's not it. OK—he who leaves his garden leaves his castle . . . or wait, I think it's his *fort*," she finished lamely, glaring at Elizabeth, who was trying unsuccessfully to control her amusement. "Whatever!" Jessica finished. "You get the picture!"

"Yes, we do, dear," Mrs. Wakefield said. "We can see it all very clearly. We know you're feeling hurt, and we know you want your sister to stay with you. But we also know that deep down, you want the best for Elizabeth, and we know you're capable of putting aside your own needs so that Elizabeth can take pleasure in this opportunity instead of feeling guilty and worried about you."

"Jess," Mr. Wakefield interjected, "sometimes we have to make sacrifices for those we love."

Jessica sighed and said nothing. She didn't want to be persuaded, but she couldn't help it—her parents' words were having an effect on her.

"Can you be happy for Elizabeth?" Mrs. Wakefield asked gently. "This is a tremendous opportunity for her."

"But I don't want us to be separated," Jessica replied, her voice small. Elizabeth shifted on the couch beside her, and Jessica saw tears glittering in her eyes.

"It will be good for both of you," Mr. Wakefield assured her.

"I know," Jessica said, her voice thick. Elizabeth's miserable expression made her insides twist, and impulsively she felt a rush of sympathy for her twin as well as a hot flush of shame for the way she had behaved. All the snippy things she'd said during her marathon gossip session with the Thetas came back to Jessica in a flow of guilty recollection.

I shouldn't have been so mean, she thought, wincing.

But she's *the mean one,* another voice inside her said. She's *the one who can't wait to fly off and leave you!*

Jessica's mind raced. Which voice should she listen to?

She stole another glance at Elizabeth, and the timid, anxious look on her face softened her. Biting her lip, her eyes as big as saucers, Elizabeth looked so vulnerable that Jessica dismissed all anger and resentment from her mind. At that moment she just wanted to make things right for Elizabeth.

"OK," Jessica said with a tender smile at her sister. "OK. She should go. It'll be good . . . for both of us."

Gratitude shone from Elizabeth's eyes, and Jessica felt a wave of warmth rising up in her chest. *I'm doing the right thing,* she thought with pleasure. Apart from making Elizabeth happy, Jessica enjoyed feeling that she had accomplished something as lofty as self-sacrifice. The very words produced a small tingle in her spine, and she basked in the glow of Elizabeth's smile and her parents' appreciative responses.

After saying her good-byes Jessica hung up and turned to Elizabeth, who was smiling broadly in spite of her tears.

"Thank you," she said softly, her voice quavering with emotion.

"You're welcome," Jessica replied.

They wrapped each other in an impulsive hug. Jessica didn't want to let go.

"What you just did really means a lot to me, Jess."

"Well, I wanted to make up for this morning," Jessica began, eager to come clean over the nasty comments she'd made to her sorority sisters. "I'm sorry I was so mean to you. I know I haven't exactly been a model of support. In fact, I even told Lila and Isabella I felt you were . . . uh . . . making the wrong decision. I told them I was concerned for you," she added, "and I, uh, shouldn't have talked about it with them before making sure it was OK with you first." *She doesn't need to know* every *little detail,* Jessica thought quickly, backtracking over her initial impulse to confess all. Elizabeth wouldn't be charmed to hear the real story, Jessica knew. She wouldn't like to hear how Jessica had snickered over Elizabeth and called her a "bossy goody two-shoes." *And anyway,* she reasoned, *an apology is an apology.*

"That's OK." Elizabeth broke free from Jessica's hug and blew her nose. "It's behind us now. And anyway," she added, "you came through

54

for me in the end. You're a great sister."

Jessica beamed at the compliment and had to admit it was well earned. Not many would be as supportive as she was in the face of such a crisis!

"One more thing," Jessica said playfully, punching Elizabeth lightly on her arm. "I know I've been slightly less than perfect over this, but you didn't have to sic Mom and Dad on me! That was really low."

"I didn't plan it that way." Elizabeth laughed. "What can I say? They got to you first!"

Jessica grinned, and the two hugged again. "OK, Liz," Jessica teased, "admit it. You fed me to the lions."

"I did not, Jessica. How dare you accuse me!" Elizabeth replied in mock indignation, grabbing a pillow from her bed and holding it above her head. "You will pay," she declared grandly.

Squealing, Jessica ducked for cover and a weapon of her own. *A pillow fight—just like old times,* she thought happily, her mood lifting.

Enjoy it while you can, another part of her said. *Soon you'll be miles apart. . . .*

Chapter Four

What to take and what to leave? Elizabeth asked herself with a sigh and a yawn. For the last couple of days she'd done nothing but sort through her belongings. Although she wasn't moving for a while yet, Elizabeth liked to prepare for things well in advance, and she thought she'd start by getting rid of all the clothes she wouldn't need in Colorado.

She held up a scruffy blue sweater patched at the arms. *Toss it,* she ordered herself sternly. "But I like this old thing!" she said aloud. After a moment's deliberation she finally tossed the sweater onto a small pile on her floor. *You're moving on to new things,* she reasoned, *so you have to let go of some of the old.*

Surveying the floor of her room, Elizabeth let out a groan. The pile for tossing was dismally small, considering she'd been at it since Sunday morning, and it was now almost evening on Monday. *How did I manage to collect so much stuff?* she wondered. *I don't even care about clothes!* She stared with amazement at the large tower of T-shirts, pants, and skirts she still had to go through. *Luckily I'm not Jessica,* she thought with a wry smile. *She'd have to hire a bulldozer just to get into her closet!*

Holding up a short maroon velvet dress, Elizabeth felt a wave of nostalgia come over her. She had last worn that dress to a dance with Tom. . . .

Toss it! she told herself firmly, but disobeying her impulse, she instead hung it back in her closet. Berating herself for her sentimentality, Elizabeth sighed heavily but made no move to take the dress back and toss it on the junk pile. Smoothing the velvet to her cheek, she closed her eyes, feeling a mixture of pain and happiness wash over her as she remembered the way she had felt the day she had bought the dress.

"It will look fabulous on you," Jessica had insisted, thumbing the rich wine fabric. "And Tom will think you're a goddess."

Elizabeth had been more hesitant about the dress. It wasn't really her style. She'd been drawn to it, but it seemed a luxury, and her practical side wasn't going for it.

"Come on, Liz!" Jessica had moaned. "For once in your life be a little dangerous, will you?"

"And I *was* dangerous." Elizabeth smiled,

remembering how she'd felt in the dress. It had changed her. If only for a night she'd acted a little crazy, dancing wildly and passionately with Tom. He'd called it The Vamp Dress after that.

"Yoo-hoo! Barbara Walters!"

"Huh?" Elizabeth looked up, dazed from her reverie, to find Jessica standing at the door of their room. She was tapping her foot impatiently, her hands on her hips.

"I called you twice by your real name, but I guess it's not working. Liz, you have to come with me right now!"

"Where?" Elizabeth's brow knitted in confusion. They didn't have any plans as far as she knew.

"Come *on*," Jessica implored, ignoring the question. "We have to get going. Hurry! Nina's waiting in the hall!"

"Wha . . . ?" But before Elizabeth had a chance to ask what was going on, Jessica grabbed her hand and dragged her from the room.

"On second thought," Jessica added, stopping to give Elizabeth a once-over, "let's make a quick stop at my vanity mirror. You look like you've been dragged backward through a bush!"

"Hey!" Elizabeth replied defensively, smoothing her hair. True, she was a bit disheveled, but what was the big deal?

"All set," Jessica trilled as she swept blush on Elizabeth's cheekbones and threw a tube of lip gloss at her. "Honestly, though, Liz, you might want to try a little face paint more often. I mean, you've got gorgeous features, but everyone needs to enhance their natural beauty." With that, Jessica snatched Elizabeth's hand and pulled her into the hallway. Nina Harper, Elizabeth's closest friend and fellow studyaholic, stood waiting.

"Hey, Nina." Elizabeth gave her friend a bemused smile as Jessica led her down the hall. Nina looked gorgeous as usual. With her smooth, dark skin, perfect figure, and big brown eyes, Nina was definitely a beauty, though she was completely unaware of this. In fact, she was almost always watching her weight—she insisted it was good discipline. "What's up?"

"Nothing that I know of," Nina replied cryptically, giving Jessica a knowing smile.

"Wait!" Elizabeth pulled free from Jessica's grip and stopped walking. "What's the big mystery?"

"OK, here's a clue—it involves old memories," Jessica said.

Old memories. Elizabeth didn't like the sound of that. Instinctively Tom came to mind, and a dreadful thought occurred to her. Surely Jessica and Nina weren't setting her up for some kind of scene with Tom in an effort to smooth things out before Elizabeth's departure? Elizabeth was horrified at the thought. They wouldn't ambush her . . . would they? Maybe *that's* why Jessica had made such a fuss over Elizabeth's appearance.

Elizabeth's eyes flicked suspiciously from Nina

to Jessica. Both wore deadpan expressions. It was hard to tell what they were up to.

"Come on," Nina urged, linking her arm through Elizabeth's.

Please let me be wrong about this, Elizabeth prayed silently, but she allowed herself to be led down the passage. It was useless trying to interrogate Nina and Jessica. There was only one way to find out what was behind those Mona Lisa smiles.

The girls stopped outside the dorm counselors' apartment, and Elizabeth breathed a sigh of relief. Whatever was going down, it was now obvious Tom wasn't involved. Elizabeth chided herself for jumping to such fantastical conclusions. *Like he would want to see me anyway,* she thought morosely.

As she walked through the door all thoughts of Tom were banished from her mind, and Elizabeth felt a surge of pleasure leap through her as she found herself looking at a banner on the wall reading Congratulations, Elizabeth! and below it a sea of familiar faces. Gathered in the small room, around a table heaped with snacks and a large chocolate cake, were Winston, Denise, Lila, Bruce, Alexandra Rollins and her boyfriend, Noah Pearson, and . . . Todd Wilkins!

Elizabeth felt her breath catch in her throat as she looked at Todd, his friendly brown eyes and cheerful smile as familiar as her own heartbeat. *He looks so upbeat,* Elizabeth thought happily. *I've hardly seen him since the funeral for Gin-Yung—*

Jessica squeezed her shoulder, interrupting her thoughts. "So what do you think?" she asked excitedly.

Elizabeth turned to Jessica with a smile of gratitude. "What a cool surprise!" she exclaimed.

"This is your life, Elizabeth Wakefield," Winston announced broadly as he gestured at a TV screen. "Sit down and watch it flash before your eyes."

"Congratulations, Liz," Todd added, folding her in a huge bear hug. "I'm really proud of you."

As Elizabeth hugged Todd back she closed her eyes, the familiar feeling of his strong arms around her immediately bringing back memories of her old feelings for him. A small tremor of sadness rippled through her body. She and Todd had such a long history together. They'd gone steady through high school but had broken up soon after they came to SVU. Their relationship wasn't meant to be; they realized this recently when an attempt at recapturing the past had ended on a sad note.

After her breakup with Tom, Elizabeth and Todd had sought comfort in rekindling their relationship. His then girlfriend, Gin-Yung Suh, was far away in London, and he had thought his feelings for her were dwindling. But when Gin-Yung had returned to Sweet Valley with a fatal brain tumor, Todd realized how wrong he had been. It took a tragic event like her hospitalization and death for Elizabeth and Todd to realize they had to go their separate ways, but Elizabeth hadn't been sure if Todd would pull through his deep depression. Until now.

Relieved, Elizabeth clasped Todd tightly, knowing he would feel her elation at his recovery and her gratitude for his lasting friendship. *We don't need words,* Elizabeth thought as she buried her head into Todd's chest. *We know each other so well.*

"Time for the show," Denise declared, handing Elizabeth a plate piled high with snacks.

"You guys are so sweet." Elizabeth felt her cheeks grow red. She wasn't used to all the attention; even though it embarrassed her a little, she definitely enjoyed it.

"To your throne, Miss Wakefield," Winston ordered, ushering Elizabeth over to an armchair.

"I don't know about this," Elizabeth murmured. "Why do I get the feeling I'm not going to like what I see?"

The others laughed and gathered around to watch.

Winston stood in front of the TV and pressed play on the VCR. "It all began a long time ago," he said as a photograph filled the screen.

Biting into a cracker loaded with salmon mousse, Elizabeth giggled as she found herself face-to-face with an image of herself at two, running away from a gleeful Jessica, who was spraying her with a garden hose.

"It wasn't always easy," Winston began as

everyone laughed. "But things picked up when she got a little older!"

The room erupted as another image filled the screen: This time a slightly older Elizabeth mugged for the camera, her arm around a pouty-looking Jessica as Elizabeth gripped Jessica's neck in a headlock.

"Where did you guys get this stuff?" Elizabeth asked, laughing.

"Your conspiring twin made it easy," Winston said.

"I just got Mom and Dad to send over the old videos and photo albums," Jessica explained.

Elizabeth pointed a jokingly accusing finger at her sister. "Schemer!"

"Studying came naturally," Winston continued.

The group cooed at a picture of Elizabeth in the first grade, standing solemnly with her back-pack in hand.

"And so did . . . looove!"

A photo of Elizabeth at thirteen holding hands with Todd on the beach flashed onto the screen. Murmurs of "How cute" from the girls and chuckles and whistles from the guys filled the air. Elizabeth felt her cheeks grow red and turned to see Todd grinning at her.

"Definitely a bad hair day, though," Jessica chimed in. "Could those bangs get any higher off your head?"

"Hey," Elizabeth yelled in mock indignation.

"If I remember correctly, those bangs were *your* doing. You were queen of the curling iron back then, Jess."

"Settle down now," Winston growled. "This is a serious event. We're chronicling the early years of a future famous journalist!"

Elizabeth rolled her eyes. "Please, Winston, you're embarrassing me!"

"That's the point!"

As another image flashed onto the screen Jessica let out a howl, which was followed by a giggling fit from Lila. Elizabeth and Jessica, wearing pink and blue full satin dresses, posed for the camera.

"Our sweet sixteen party!" Elizabeth exclaimed. "Look how sweet we look, Jess!"

"Speak for yourself," Jessica replied. "What were we thinking with those dresses? We look like cupcakes! And our hair . . . ugh! I can't believe that was just a few years ago!"

"And the frosty blue eye shadow," Lila added. "Definitely a fashion faux pas."

"Funny," Jessica retorted coolly. "I seem to remember borrowing that makeup from *you*, Li!"

"Well, I think they both look adorable," Alex said. "Especially compared to me at sixteen!"

Winston clapped. "Speaking of which . . ."

A picture of Elizabeth and Alex—or Enid, as she was known in those days—filled the screen. They were hugging each other in the Wakefields' kitchen.

"Yuck!" Alex squealed, covering her eyes. "Look at that blob! Hello, Ten-Ton Tessa! Make it go away, Win."

Elizabeth smiled wistfully at Alex, but Alex didn't seem to notice. *We used to be so close,* Elizabeth thought. But that was before Enid decided to make herself into someone more "exciting" and changed her name to Alexandra. Now she was a Theta and didn't have much in common with Elizabeth anymore. *But we still have the past,* Elizabeth caught herself thinking. *And nothing can ever change that. . . .*

A warm pressure at her shoulder broke Elizabeth's train of thought. She turned her head to see Todd smiling at her and pointing at the TV screen.

"When it comes to Liz," Winston warbled, "looove lasts!"

A picture of Elizabeth and Todd dancing at their Sweet Valley High junior prom sent a bittersweet arrow through Elizabeth's chest.

As she lowered her eyes from the image of herself in a shimmering pale lavender gown, her arms around Todd, Elizabeth smiled to herself. Todd would always be a special person in her life, and she knew that she meant a lot to him too. His being next to her right now proved that they had a lasting bond, no matter what the future held.

At that moment a shot of Tom and Elizabeth in the WSVU office came onto the screen.

"We chart the real beginnings of the reporter

at work," Winston said. "As usual, mixing business with pleasure," he teased, "a pattern she might just follow in Colorado with a certain victim whom I shall not name!"

The others laughed, and Winston gave Elizabeth a knowing wink. Elizabeth tried to smile, but a flash of pain cut through her chest as she looked at Tom's face in full-color close-up on the TV. *If only Tom could be supportive too,* she thought with regret. It would mean so much if he would bury the hatchet and wish her well with her new future. But remembering the way his face had twisted in anger just three days earlier, Elizabeth knew it wasn't going to happen.

Lifting her chin, Elizabeth concentrated instead on the faces around her. Winston was clearly enjoying himself, kidding around in his usual fashion, playing to the crowd. The others talked and laughed among themselves, wisecracking at the video and making the usual amount of noise.

Elizabeth felt so comfortable with all of them. They'd known each other for so long. Would she find such good friends in Colorado? *Yes, you will,* she told herself. *It'll be a challenge, but you'll find your place.* Still, Elizabeth remembered with a mixture of pleasure and sadness what her grandmother always said: "New friends are silver, but old friends are gold."

At that thought Elizabeth felt tears fill her eyes. Seeing her memories rising up before her in full color was simply too intense.

Don't be silly, she chided herself, annoyed at her lack of control. *This is a celebration, not a funeral!* Composing herself, Elizabeth took a deep breath and brushed her tears away quickly, hoping that no one had noticed.

"Liz's gothic phase! Dig that outfit!" Winston whooped at the picture that now filled the screen: Elizabeth dressed as a bat for a Halloween party.

Winston was having a ball. Cracking jokes and being in the spotlight was his favorite thing, and this little act in honor of Elizabeth was no exception. Winston had jumped at the chance to put the video together and surprise his friend, and he had to admit, he'd outdone himself on the wit front this evening. Everyone had laughed at his video narration, making Winston feel better than he had in days. *Nothing like a little comic relief when you need it,* he thought. Winston needed this distraction to take him away from worrying about Denise's debt. He'd been racking his brains for almost three days now, and still he couldn't come up with a solution to her credit card problem.

Oops! Winston had gotten so lost in thought, he hadn't noticed that the picture on the TV had switched from the Halloween photo to a shot of Elizabeth and Jessica posing in their Jeep outside Dickenson. Winston had taped Barbra Streisand's "The Way We Were" for the background, and the laughter died down as everyone grew reflective to the strains of the melody.

"Memories," Winston interjected softly. "You'll always have great memories, Liz." He looked over at his old friend and saw a tear streak down her face, glinting in the dark.

"Looking back, I still remember . . . the way we were. . . ."

The song ended, and Winston heard Jessica give a small hiccuping sob. Just then a not altogether flattering close-up of Elizabeth, mouth open, giving a broadcast report, appeared on the screen alongside a loud version of the song "Fame."

"But heck," Winston yelled, "enough already! I'm a reporter, and I'm gonna live forever!" He sang along loudly and tunelessly.

Everyone erupted into raucous laughter again, and Winston felt a glow of pride. He'd had to pull some strings to get that clip from WSVU without going through Watts, who he knew wouldn't jump in to help out on any project involving Elizabeth. Judging by the group's reaction, it had been worth the effort. But Elizabeth's head was down, and Jessica didn't look too happy either.

"Hey!" Winston exclaimed. "Don't you Wakefields start getting mushy on us now! Liz," he added gently, noting Elizabeth's sober expression, "do you want me to stop the video?"

"What are you talking about, Egbert?" Jessica cut in. "I for one am *perfectly* fine. Keep it rolling!"

"Well, *I'm* not crying," Elizabeth added hotly.

69

"You guys know me better than that. *Jess* is the emotional one, not me!"

Whoa! Winston thought. *We're in for a show-down now!*

Jessica flashed Elizabeth an angry look. "Well, well," she said, sarcasm dripping from her words, "aren't we just *so* levelheaded and mature, Liz. Wish *I* could control myself like you can. But then I guess that would make me an ice block too!"

The room fell into awkward silence, and Winston looked from Jessica to Elizabeth. Elizabeth's cheeks blazed angrily. Winston hadn't seen her in a temper very often, but he could tell that she was *really* furious. Obviously something was up between them, and it was going to erupt right now.

"I think you've just proved my point, Jessica," Elizabeth began frostily. "Clearly you can't keep your emotions in check. You'd think you'd have learned when to shut your mouth by now, but I guess some things never change!"

All right, Egbert, Winston told himself, *do what you do best. Crack a joke!* "Speaking of cake," Winston began in a loud voice, "and I know we weren't, but we should have been—let's all take a quick cake break and partake of the wondrous creation cooked up for us on this splendiferous occasion by none other than the charming and unusually gifted Ms. Denise Waters, also known for her association with an SVU celebrity of the first order, your resident doofus, Winston Egbert!"

70

Winston gave an exaggerated bow, and Bruce and Noah chuckled, but the joke didn't seem to have had any effect on Jessica or Elizabeth. They hadn't moved from their positions and were still staring each other down in an ugly standoff.

Sighing, Winston waited for the inevitable fit of hysteria from Jessica. Knowing her, she was about to scream at Elizabeth for a good few minutes and flounce out of the room with typical drama.

"Winston, everyone, thank you," Elizabeth said, her voice low and shaking. With that she spun on her heel and rushed out of the room. As an uneasy hush took over, everyone, Winston included, traded shocked looks. It wasn't like Elizabeth to be so fazed by Jessica, but this time she really seemed stung. Obviously there was more to this tiff than met the eye.

"Uh, sorry, you guys," Jessica mumbled, breaking the silence. "I guess I'd better go too."

Jessica left the room, and Lila, Noah, Alex, and Nina left soon after. "Well!" Winston raised an eyebrow as Denise and the guys stood around awkwardly. "Cake, anyone?"

Chapter Five

"Elizabeth, *what* is *wrong* with you?"

Elizabeth said nothing, and Jessica hurried to catch up with her. Her sister was marching ahead at an angry pace, her ponytail bobbing with each step.

What right does she *have to be so ticked off?* Jessica thought, smarting. *After all, she insulted me first!* Jessica felt a flame of anger burst inside her chest as she fell in step beside her sister. Elizabeth didn't even look up. She simply carried on moving, her eyes fixed ahead.

"Elizabeth!" Jessica repeated loudly, but still she was ignored. "*Now* who's the emotional one? Don't you think the pot just called the kettle black in there?"

Elizabeth slowed down at that comment, and Jessica smiled triumphantly. *Quite a coup,* she congratulated herself. *Even Elizabeth can't deny I scored a point there!*

"Jessica, I don't want to talk to you right now. Please leave me alone!"

"What?" Jessica's mouth dropped open. Elizabeth was being unusually pigheaded. Even Jessica had to admit to herself that when it came to arguments, the end result was usually *Jessica* stalking off in a huff and *Elizabeth* trying to make her come around.

She really is *acting weird,* Jessica mused before her indignation returned. *Well, I'm not going to let her push me around, even if she does think she's a big shot now.*

"I don't care whether you're in the mood or not, Elizabeth. I'm going to talk to you, and that's just the way it is."

"Fine!" Elizabeth whirled around and faced Jessica. "So speak! Tell me what you have to say—but if you just want to heap on more insults, then don't bother opening your mouth. I've had just about all I can handle these past three days."

"*Insults?*" Jessica spat, feeling her cheeks grow hot with rage. "It was *you* who humiliated me at the party in front of everyone. *You* started it!"

"I wasn't cruel, Jessica," Elizabeth replied, lowering her voice. "I just said you were emotional, which is true."

Jessica glared at Elizabeth, bristling with anger. But as she stared her down, she couldn't help noticing her sister's appearance. Even aside from her angry expression, she didn't look too good.

There were dark circles under her eyes, and her usually glowing complexion was ashy.

Something's up with her, Jessica reflected. *But whatever it is, she doesn't have to take it out on me!*

Jessica's frustration returned, and she sucked in a deep breath. Who did Elizabeth think she was, acting all pinched and schoolteachery, standing there folding her arms and telling Jessica off in her high-and-mighty voice?

"OK," Jessica replied, "so I'm the emotional one." She took a step toward Elizabeth, narrowing her eyes. "Fine! At least I'm not a cold fish like *you.*"

"What's that supposed to mean?" Elizabeth replied defensively.

"Nothing seems to move you!" Jessica shot back. "You said *I* was the emotional one. What's *that* supposed to mean? Are you saying you're *not*? What are you trying to prove, Elizabeth? That you have no feelings?"

"I do too have feelings!" Elizabeth bit her lip and turned away from Jessica, a hurt expression on her face.

"Then what are they?" Jessica cried. "I'd really like to know!"

Elizabeth remained silent and looked away. All of a sudden a thought occurred to Jessica.

This is not about me.

She could see that Elizabeth was in pain and was trying to hide it. *If she's trying to hide it, it*

75

must *have something to do with Tom,* she reasoned. Lately every problem and every depression Elizabeth went through began with Tom Watts. *Wasn't it a fight between Elizabeth and Tom that made her think of leaving in the first place?*

Jessica cocked her head, trying to make sense of all the details. Clearly Elizabeth was torn; on the one hand, she was happy to be leaving Tom and all her bad memories behind, and on the other, she was miserable. Yes, the more she thought about it, the more Jessica became convinced that Elizabeth was using the journalism school opportunity as a reason, but in actual fact it was just an excuse to run away from Tom once and for all.

And I'm the one who has to suffer! Jessica concluded numbly. *Liz is leaving* me *because of some jerk!* The thought hit Jessica like a slap in the face. Was this true?

"I've got one more question for you, and you'd better listen up because this is something you should be asking *yourself.*" Jessica tossed her hair and fixed her eyes on Elizabeth, who still wouldn't meet her gaze. "Are you running away *with* Scott so you can run away *from* Tom?"

Elizabeth felt her breath catch in her throat. Jessica's question had left her at a loss for words. With shaking fingers she concentrated instead on unlocking the door to room 28. As she swung open the door Elizabeth pushed her way inside, aware of Jessica at her elbow, radiating with satisfaction at having pinched a nerve.

And she has, Elizabeth thought. Still, neither Tom nor Scott had anything to do with her decision to go to journalism school!

But they sure helped, a voice inside her head taunted. She shook her head to silence it.

"I'm not running away, Jessica," Elizabeth said firmly as she walked toward her side of the room. "I don't know why you just can't seem to get it, but going to Denver is an opportunity I'm *taking*, not a safety net I'm falling into."

With Jessica at her heels Elizabeth did an about-face and headed for the kitchenette. She filled a mug with water and put it in the microwave, her movements brisk, and selected a fragrant bag of chamomile tea. *Something to relax me,* she thought grimly as she set the timer for three minutes. *Though after all the dramas I've been having lately, it'll take more than this little tea bag to calm me down.*

"Are you sure about that?" Jessica raised an eyebrow.

Elizabeth busied herself with the tea. "Quite sure," she answered. Jessica was really getting on her nerves—more so than usual. "If you weren't so stubborn and selfish," Elizabeth added, "you'd see that I really am taking on a challenge—and for the right reasons. But I guess you're too busy nursing your own wounds to think about mine."

Her voice was confident and calm, but her heart was hammering at her chest. All this talk was only making her doubt her decision again, and she didn't feel like going through yet another soul search. *And anyway,* Elizabeth thought in irritation, *who gave Jessica the right to question my motives? It's a little rich coming from her, considering all the bad moves she's made in* her *life!*

"Well—"

"Listen, Jessica," Elizabeth snapped, dropping the tea bag into the steaming mug of water. "I'm tired, I've had a long day, and I think you should lay off."

"I'm just trying to help you," Jessica replied smoothly. "You seem a little confused—*deluded,* maybe—and I think you need my advice."

"Deluded?" Elizabeth shrieked, spilling hot water onto her hand. "Ouch," she breathed, slamming down the mug. "You *must* be joking. How many times have you made important decisions and completely ignored *my* advice? And with drastic consequences, I might add!"

"Like when?" Jessica challenged.

"Boy, do you have selective amnesia," Elizabeth exclaimed. "Like when you moved in with and then *married* Mike McAllery! If I remember correctly, you didn't even ask for my advice then, let alone take it. And that's just one of many times."

Jessica looked huffy but was obviously struggling

to formulate a retort. Elizabeth couldn't help gloating. It was true—Jessica *had* done many crazy things in the name of spontaneity and given Elizabeth plenty of headaches. How many countless times had she had to cover for Jessica, all because of some rash impulse? Like her crazy marriage to Mike McAllery. Elizabeth shivered, recalling how worried and shocked she'd been when Jessica had fallen under his spell. Dangerous, womanizing Mike had completely captivated Jessica, and she'd gone to him like a lamb to the slaughter.

"My marriage was annulled," Jessica replied feebly.

"No comment," Elizabeth said. Luckily for Jessica, she had people to bail her out of her mistakes. And there had been big ones. *Yet she has the nerve to call me on this,* Elizabeth fumed. *A decision that I made with a great deal of thought and responsibility.* Clearly Jessica was just being immature and causing trouble. *I thought we'd sorted this all out earlier anyway,* Elizabeth thought with annoyance. *Why are we going through it all again?*

"Jessica, I've made a responsible, informed decision," Elizabeth announced self-importantly. "Remember, you promised Mom and Dad you'd support me one hundred percent. Now if you really care about me, I know you will." Satisfied with her speech, Elizabeth moved over to her bed and sank down onto it gratefully, taking a long sip from her mug. As far as she was concerned, there was nothing further to be said on the subject, and she was going to drink her tea—in peace and quiet, hopefully—and get some rest after yet another emotional day.

"If you really cared about *me*," Jessica replied venomously, her voice slow and precise, "then you wouldn't be running away because of some stupid guy!"

Elizabeth winced. Each of Jessica's words stabbed her like small, white-hot needles. Jessica really knew how to get to her. Elizabeth opened her mouth to speak, then thought better of it and shut it. Some accusations weren't meant to be dignified with a response.

Jessica has a point, a little voice whispered insidiously inside her. *Don't deny it. This* is *all about Tom, and you're just kidding yourself.*

As soon as the notion occurred to her Elizabeth blocked it. It was nonsense anyway! *Leaving Tom is an added bonus, not a motive!* she reasoned.

Elizabeth took a long sip of her tea and looked up to see Jessica struggling with a small designer bag. "What are you doing?" Elizabeth asked as Jessica balled up a pale peach minidress and shoved it into the bag.

"What does it look like?" Jessica grunted, forcing a pair of tan suede mules into the side pocket. "I'm packing."

"I can see that, Jess," Elizabeth replied calmly.

"No need to be sarcastic. But *why* are you packing?"

"Because I'm going out!" Jessica flipped her hair in annoyance and stood up, swinging a leather jacket over her shoulder.

"Where are you going? It's almost nine o'clock." Elizabeth couldn't help being amused, and a small smile flickered at the corner of her mouth. Jessica really was *so* impulsive and impractical. Trust her to stuff her clothes into a tiny patent leather bag rather than suffer the inelegance of a roomier backpack.

"Call me crazy, but I don't find nine o'clock to be dangerously late," Jessica retorted. "But then again, we all know I'm not the practical, level-headed one of us two."

"Oh, Jessica." Elizabeth sighed. "Can't you just give it up already? I'm tired of arguing with you."

Ignoring Elizabeth, Jessica grabbed her keys and made for the door.

"Where are you going?"

"To Nick's," Jessica answered, stopping to pick up a pair of socks that had rolled out of her bag.

"*Now* look who's running away!"

The door slammed in response. Elizabeth sighed heavily and lay down, her eyes fixed on the ceiling. The sudden silence of the room seemed oppressive, and after a moment Elizabeth sat up again. The tea hadn't worked, and she didn't feel remotely sleepy. Quite the opposite: Her brain had begun ticking again, and her stomach fluttered nervously as she heard Jessica's voice in her head.

Running away because of some stupid guy . . .

Was she right?

Elizabeth sat up in alarm. *Is that what I'm doing?* She took a deep breath and realized she could no longer afford to ignore these burning questions. She *had* to allow her mind to explore them. Until now she'd been pushing these thoughts down as soon as they popped up in her head. Now was the time to face up to things. She had to be honest and cross-examine herself. *You can't run away from yourself,* she thought wryly. *But are you running away from Tom? Is that what Denver is really all about?*

She *was* excited about transferring to DCIR, and she was flattered to have been asked, but she had to admit that if she wasn't so unhappy, leaving Sweet Valley would never have crossed her mind even for a second. Elizabeth knew that other great opportunities would come along, whether she sought them out or not. After all, she had had a pretty exciting reporting career at SVU anyway, and good stories and hard work weren't particular to DCIR, even if they did have the best journalism program in the country.

Jessica's right, Elizabeth thought, her hands beginning to tremble. She couldn't deny it anymore, even to herself.

I am *running away.*

Standing up, Elizabeth put her thumbs to her

temples and squeezed. All this thinking was giving her a headache. *It doesn't matter anyway*, she thought. *Thinking about this is worthless. There's nothing I can do now. I'm going to Colorado, for better or for worse!*

"Oh, Nick," Jessica sobbed. "It's useless. She's *leaving* me!" With a loud moan she fell into Nick's arms and cried onto his flannel shirt. She felt wretched, although she did have to admit that emotional breakdowns around Nick had definite pluses; he really did have a chest worth crying on, and his strong, powerful arms were pillars of strength in more than one sense—they made her feel safe and loved too.

"Don't worry, angel," Nick murmured into Jessica's hair. "Everything will be all right, I promise."

Jessica could almost believe him. Soft candlelight gave Nick's living room a warm, romantic glow, and the thick white carpet, along with the soft leather sofa where they lay curled up together, made Jessica feel as if she were floating on a cloud, far above Sweet Valley and all the problems of the world.

"I don't know about that. Elizabeth can be pretty stubborn, you know."

Nick chuckled. "Let's see," he teased, "who does that remind me of . . . ?"

"Nick!" Jessica snapped, slapping his arm lightly. "Stop joking around. This is serious stuff!"

She sighed heavily, shifting in Nick's arms. *At least I still have him,* Jessica consoled herself. And Nick would help her out with this Elizabeth problem, Jessica knew. He had always been there for her when she'd needed him most.

Turning toward Nick, Jessica traced his strong jaw and high cheekbones with the tip of a finger, thinking for the hundredth time how lucky she was to have him. He really was a dream come true.

Almost hadn't come true . . .

A chill shot up her spine as Jessica remembered how she had felt back when it seemed as if their relationship—and her whole life—were doomed. Nick, working undercover as an SVU student, had been tracking a drug deal and mistakenly arrested Jessica. Jessica shivered, thinking back to her desperation in prison: the dirty cell, the terrifying inmates, and a cocaine-trafficking charge hanging over her. But none of it had compared with losing Nick. Thank goodness he had finally believed her and caught the real culprit, scheming Celine Boudreaux.

At one point during the ordeal Jessica had lost faith, convinced that she was going to spend her life behind bars with bad food and bad prison fashion. Thankfully Nick had come through for her in the end and saved her from hell. Looking up at him, Jessica considered again how lucky she was to have such a fabulous boyfriend.

"Come here," Jessica murmured seductively,

grazing Nick's cheek with her lips. As Nick's mouth met hers she felt the stress of the past few hours melt away. "Mmmm," Jessica sighed as his mouth moved to her neck. Nick was an incredible kisser, and the fiery trail of kisses moving back up from her neck to her chin was driving Jessica wild. *A few more minutes of this and I'll forget all about Elizabeth . . . just like she's forgotten about me,* Jessica thought.

A moment passed, and Jessica sat up. Despite the warmth of Nick's hands at her back and his full, deep kisses, it was no use. She couldn't stop thinking about Elizabeth.

"Jess," Nick groaned. "What's up?"

"I'm sorry, Nick. But there are more important things to do than lying around kissing all night."

"It never seemed to bother you before," Nick teased, smiling up at her lazily. "A week ago a volcano could have erupted and you wouldn't have noticed." Gently Nick began to stroke Jessica's arm. "C'mon," he purred. "Don't get yourself too worked up over this thing with Liz. Why don't you just forget about it for a while?"

Jessica tossed her head angrily. "Easy for you to say," she snapped. "You're not the one whose twin sister is bailing on her! You're not the one left behind to pick up the pieces!"

"Calm down, Jess." Nick touched Jessica's hand, but she shrugged him off impatiently.

"I will *not* calm down! In case you haven't noticed,

I'm going through a *major* crisis here. I'd appreciate a little support, if it isn't too much to ask."

"OK, OK." Nick sighed, a smile twitching at his lips. "What can I do?"

"Help me find a way to stop her from leaving," Jessica wailed, tears welling up under her eyelids. Focusing her big blue-green eyes on Nick, Jessica did her best to look completely helpless, knowing that this would get Nick going. He liked nothing more than to rescue her.

"OK, Jess," Nick began. "I have a plan."

"What?" Jessica widened her eyes with enthusiasm. *Thank goodness I'm in love with a cop,* she thought happily. *They're so practical! Not even two minutes and the guy has a plan!*

"But you may not like what I have to say."

"Oh?" Jessica frowned. If she wouldn't like the plan, then it couldn't be much of a plan, now, could it?

"I think you should let Liz go—"

"Let her *go?"* Jessica's voice was sharp. *Is he on drugs? I'm not going to let her go! I depend on Liz. Nick of all people should know that!*

"Hear me out for a second, Jess. If you stand in Elizabeth's way, she could hold it against you for the rest of your life. Now, do you want that?"

Jessica bit her lip. He did have a point. *If I made enough of a fuss, maybe Liz would stay, but she would definitely never let me forget about it. She'd spend the rest of our lives playing the martyr. . . .*

She could just picture it. She saw Elizabeth, thirty years from now, being asked why she never made anything of herself. "Well," Elizabeth would reply, "I had a chance to go to the best journalism school in America. But who was going to make sure my sister woke up on time for class every morning?"

I guess Nick's right, she thought morosely. But why did everything have to be so difficult with Elizabeth? Why couldn't they just turn back the clock and be young again, with no thoughts of the world beyond the Dairi Burger and their own backyard?

"OK." Jessica sighed, beginning to feel guilty for the harsh words she'd said to Elizabeth earlier. "I'll stop trying to get Liz to stay."

"Good girl." Nick kissed the top of her head. "You're doing the right thing. And speaking of change," he added, "I've decided to extend my leave of absence from the force. Since I rocked my college entrance exams, I'd be crazy not to."

Jessica could only open and close her mouth like a dying fish in response. She couldn't speak. *I don't believe this,* she thought as a hard, tight knot formed in her stomach. *After all I've gone through in the last few days, he has to go and bring up his stupid college thing!*

Nick had been making noises about leaving the force and going to college as a prelaw major, and he'd even gone as far as taking the college entrance exams. But Jessica never truly believed that when push came to shove, he'd leave his exciting job on the force for pinstripes and textbooks.

Even though she dreaded the thought of something happening to Nick in the line of duty, she still couldn't help feeling that college would turn Nick into a different guy. Maybe he'd even evolve into a major nerd. She'd seen it happen while he was preparing to take his exams. At first she'd thought it was kind of cute, but the cuteness factor wore off *real* quick.

Jessica gulped, picturing Nick holding a stack of thick, boring books, chatting to a cluster of legal types like her brother, Steven. She shoved the image aside—it was too depressing to contemplate.

"I definitely need to do this," Nick continued, his voice breaking into Jessica's thoughts. "So maybe I'll sit in on a few classes at SVU, see how it feels, and go from there. What do you think?"

Jessica felt a hot ball of anger surge through her chest. What was this? Since when was everyone so gung ho on change? Couldn't they all just stop for a moment and think—*really* think—about what they were doing?

"So what do you think?" Nick repeated impatiently.

What do you want? A pat on the back? Jessica wondered. Of *course* she thought it was a horrible idea. Now her boyfriend would be just like everyone else's—taking classes, studying, hanging out at frat parties . . . going to the library! *Ugh!* No more of the suave sophistication that was Nick Fox, undercover cop.

Jessica had opened her mouth to give Nick her opinion on the matter when she was interrupted by a voice from inside her. *And if you stand in his way, won't he also end up resenting* you? it asked.

She bit her lip. It was all too frustrating. But it didn't seem as if she had much choice.

"I think . . . that's a great idea, Nick!" Jessica thought her bright, false voice betrayed the way she was really feeling, but Nick didn't seem to notice as he enfolded her in a tight embrace.

"I'm glad you think so, honey," he responded, giving her a kiss on her shoulder.

I'm losing him, Jessica thought sadly. *The Nick I love is leaving me too.* . . . She wound her arms tighter around his neck, as if doing this could keep him the way he was right now, here, forever. A tear rolled down Jessica's cheek, but she brushed it away quickly. *I'll just make the most of the time I* do *have,* she consoled herself, trying to be brave. But there wasn't much time left, especially for Elizabeth. She'd have to make every second count and turn the rest of the semester into a nonstop party—

A party! Jessica suddenly remembered how she'd angrily told her sorority sisters that she wanted to throw Elizabeth a good-bye party.

Considering how she felt now, she no longer wanted to do it out of spite, but out of love. Her sister had looked so happy when she'd walked in on the little surprise party she'd planned with Winston that evening. Just imagine how she'd react to a big bash in her honor! Jessica brightened visibly at the very idea. It would be the perfect way to show Elizabeth she cared, and it would also be the most fun Jessica would have in weeks. Naturally it would have to be huge. *And I could wear my new bias-cut Valentino dress,* Jessica thought with excitement.

You mean Valentino knockoff! Somehow Lila's voice had cut into Jessica's fantasy, and Jessica made a face.

Amazing. Lila doesn't even have to be in the room and she can still irk me! she mused.

"Hey, where did you go?" Nick asked, combing his fingers softly through Jessica's hair.

"Huh? Oh, I was just thinking about Lila," Jessica replied.

"Lila?"

"Yeah, and the rest of the Thetas too."

"Well, banish them from your brain and concentrate on me instead," Nick whispered as he began to plant small kisses along her hairline.

"Sorry, Nick." Jessica pushed him away gently and stood up. "I'm afraid I have to make a phone call. Emergency Theta business!"

Ignoring the way Nick was frowning, Jessica

moved to the phone and began dialing Isabella's number, her spirits lifting. *We'll have to get moving with the invitations. And then there's the catering. It will have to be properly catered . . . and of course I'll need new shoes. . . . After all, it'll be the party to end all parties!*

In a way, it was.

_____

One more minute of this and they'll have to put me in a mental institution! Elizabeth thought as she slammed the paperback she was reading to the floor with a frustrated scream. It was no use. She'd been reading the same line for the past half hour and hadn't taken in a word of it. Her mind had been spinning over and over like a Ferris wheel, questions tumbling over one another faster and faster until she thought she would be sick.

Sighing, Elizabeth turned onto her side, pulling her sheet up under her chin. Sleep was out of the question despite the chamomile tea. *A lot of good that did me,* she thought ruefully. *Maybe someone substituted Sleepy Chamomile with Atomic Zinger!*

Groaning, Elizabeth flipped over onto her other side and stared miserably at the collage of photographs on the wall in front of her. A flash of guilt made her wince as her eye caught a snapshot of herself with Jessica, sharing a brownie, their faces smeared with chocolate.

But look how happy we are, she reflected. All evening thoughts of Jessica and leaving had plagued her. Images from Winston's video kept flitting into Elizabeth's mind, and she felt haunted by her own memories. And now she couldn't even sleep because her eyes had fixed on yet another stack of moments to remember! When would she stop second-guessing herself?

You already know it's too late to back off, Elizabeth told herself. *After all, the whole world knows you're leaving. You've made your choice, and you have to stick with it.*

But would Jessica be all right without her? Elizabeth couldn't shake the image she had of Jessica leaving earlier for Nick's. Her eyes lacked their usual luster, and she had looked so jittery and distressed.

She couldn't wait to get to Nick's, Elizabeth thought miserably. *Maybe she's right—maybe she won't survive without me.* Secretly, deep down inside, Elizabeth couldn't help taking a pinch of pleasure in the situation. It was nice to be so loved and to feel so needed.

Hey, who are you kidding? she chided herself, smiling ruefully. *Look at the facts! Jessica's out with someone who loves her and whom she loves, while you're alone at home. Jessica will be fine. It's* you *you should be worrying about!*

Elizabeth sat up and threw off the covers. Jamming her feet into her slippers, she glanced at the clock. It was only 10 P.M. Still early enough to call a friend and go out. *That's what I need,* Elizabeth told herself. *To get out of my head for a while before I go stir-crazy.* Pulling a sweatshirt over her head, Elizabeth walked over to the phone. Maybe Scott would want to get some decaf at the Java Joint. Elizabeth dialed Scott's number, already cheered at the prospect of company, but after the fourth ring her spirits fell. When she got his machine, Elizabeth hung up. Maybe he was asleep or already out. Either way, there didn't seem to be much point in leaving a message.

She thought of calling Nina but knew she wouldn't be in. She'd be hitting the books in the library. Elizabeth smiled. Nina was the one person who outstudied her. She was focused to the point of obsession.

Who else can I call? Elizabeth sat scrolling mentally through names. An unexpected one stuck in her head. Tom. At the thought of him her heart began to pound. *Wouldn't* that *be funny!* she thought humorlessly. *"Hi, Tom, just wondering if you want to shoot the breeze at the Java Joint!"* Not likely. Not unless she, Elizabeth, was actually dreaming and woke up to find that the whole Tom saga had simply been a nightmare, and in reality they were still the number-one loving couple on campus.

But maybe you should call, she couldn't help thinking. The idea was completely crazy, but once it entered her head, Elizabeth couldn't let go of it. It *would* be insane, irrational, and spontaneous. *All the things I'm not*, she told herself. But it *would* be wonderful to smooth things over with Tom.

For a moment Elizabeth fantasized about clearing the air with him. She saw them talking, hesitantly at first, but then finally coming to terms with their past. Perhaps it wasn't too late to bury the hatchet. And it would mean so much if Tom ended up wishing her well.

Slowly Elizabeth placed a shaking hand on the phone. Her heart began to beat even more rapidly, and she felt as if it would explode out of her chest. *I'm going to do it*, she told herself. *I'll do it now, while I'm here alone and it's nighttime and I'm feeling wild*. If it were morning or if Jessica were around, Elizabeth knew she'd never have the guts to make the call.

Swallowing hard, she closed her fingers around the receiver, ready to dial Tom's number for the first time in ages.

Ring!

The phone vibrated in her hand. The loud ring startled Elizabeth, sending shock waves through her whole body. Who could it be? *Could it be . . . Tom?* she thought in excitement. *Could he, right this second, have had the same idea as me?* Even though the odds were about a zillion to one, Elizabeth felt she just might be right.

"H-Hello?" Her voice shook in anticipation.

"Hi."

It was a male voice. Elizabeth swallowed, unable to speak.

"Jen? It's Michael."

Elizabeth's spirits plummeted, and she felt as if a huge boulder had just fallen into her stomach. "I'm sorry," she began, her voice toneless, "but . . . you have the wrong number."

After hanging up, Elizabeth felt a wave of disappointment wash over her. She stared out the window at the pale moon. Her moment of bravery had been cut short by the misplaced phone call. She couldn't get up the nerve to call Tom now.

What were you thinking anyway? she scolded herself bitterly. *He doesn't care about you—and neither does anyone else. Face it, everyone you know is out forgetting about you already.*

Just then the phone rang again and Elizabeth grabbed it, feeling tears of helplessness in the back of her throat. *Didn't that guy get it?* she wondered in frustration and anger. "Wrong number!" she snapped.

"How strange!" Jessica chirped. "You sound *so* much like my sister, and the last time I checked, this was *my* phone number too!"

"Oh . . . hi, Jess. Sorry about that." Elizabeth smiled faintly at the sound of Jessica's voice; it was the bright, friendly Jessica she hadn't heard in ages. Feeling a sudden flood of warmth, Elizabeth took a deep breath and began speaking, words tumbling over one another in a stream of emotion. "Look, Jess, I'm really sorry about everything—"

"Don't say another word," Jessica interrupted. "*I'm* the one who should be apologizing."

"Oh, don't—"

"No, I'm really, really sorry for the way I've been acting. And I want to make it up to you."

Elizabeth felt her tears subside, and she smiled with relief. "Thank you."

"Don't thank me just yet—because I'm going to throw you a *huge* party, Liz," Jessica continued. "And by huge I mean everyone who's anyone is gonna be there—even some of those nobodies you're friends with, I suppose," she added.

Elizabeth laughed. *This* was the Jessica she knew!

"It's going to be a great big send-off for you, Liz, before you begin your new and fabulous life! Of course," she added, "it won't be, like, a *real* good-bye party since you aren't leaving for a while yet. It'll be more like a celebration, I guess. You'll never guess what I've got planned!" Jessica paused to take an audible breath. "From catering to music, it's going to be totally incredible. Because you deserve it."

Elizabeth giggled again. Jessica's enthusiasm was infectious, and a party would be fun. As Jessica began to reel off names of people she was going to invite, Elizabeth felt her loneliness shrinking.

"But remember, Liz, this is a party, not a journalism convention, so that means *glamour* as opposed to *granola* and *flirting*, not *fact checking!*"

"Jessica!" Elizabeth laughed. "You underestimate me. Just because I don't spend all my time shopping doesn't mean I don't like to dress up once in a while."

"Good! Now I want you to think *fabrics* tonight. Skirt lengths, heel heights, you know, the real deal. And then we'll go shopping. You *must* get something new, Liz. You don't have anything decent to wear in your closet! I checked it out today, and it's sadly lacking. So we'll make it Friday afternoon, but that doesn't give us much time if we're going to have the party on Friday night, right? Which reminds me, I have to call Lila and talk music. Bye!"

The line hastily clicked, and Elizabeth found herself smiling at the wall. *Thank goodness for Jessica,* she thought. *If it weren't for her phone call, there'd be enough tears here to flood the hallway.*

Still smiling, Elizabeth went back to bed, her mind fixed on the party. *That'll cheer me up,* she thought. *Even if it is a bit too soon for good-byes . . .*

"Arrggh!" Denise rolled her eyes in annoyance and flopped back onto her futon when the phone rang.

"There you go," Winston said, gesturing at the phone. "One of the girls, no doubt, calling to give you a complete rundown on the latest globally significant events. Such as the decimation of the rain forests. Or Elizabeth and Jessica's tiff. Aren't you going to answer it?" he asked when Denise made no move to get off the futon.

"No. You get it." Denise looked worried. "It's probably a collection agent. If it is, tell them I'm not in."

For a moment Winston felt anxious. He still hadn't come up with a plan to help Denise. *Oh, heck,* he thought with a grin, *why take it all so seriously? We'll sort Denise out later. But* this *could be fun!* He gave Denise a thumbs-up. "Don't worry, Denise, I'll give that collection agent a run for her money—no pun intended!" Clearing his throat, Winston picked up the phone and with a fake foreign accent began to speak. "Miss Waters's estate!" he said loudly, ignoring Denise's frantic hand signals.

"Yes, may I speak with Denise Waters, please?" Winston recognized the polite but cool voice on the other end. It was the collection agent he'd heard before on Denise's machine.

"I am very sorry," said Winston. "But she is not here, I don't think. I look, I no find."

"Pardon me?" The woman on the other end sounded mystified. Winston stifled a chuckle. This was right up his alley.

"I say, no Miss Waters in the house!" he repeated, making a silly face at Denise, who rolled her eyes back at him.

"And to whom am I speaking?" the voice inquired, a note of impatience creeping in.

"Me, I am Pierre Chardonnay, *exterminateur* extraordinaire!"

Denise giggled, muffling the sound with a pillow.

"Very, very many roaches in this dorm," Winston added. "I come to exterminate!"

"Really," the voice replied, sounding skeptical. "At this time of night?"

"Emergency roach problem!" Winston almost cracked up. This was good!

"Well, if you see Ms. Waters, would you give her a message?"

"Sure, I give her massage!" Winston replied, ignoring Denise as she shook her head wildly.

"Will you tell her to call Ms. Arlene at the California Commission for Student Assistance?" the woman asked.

Winston pretended to take down a number. "Very good," he said, and hung up. "How was that?" He jumped onto the futon beside Denise, pleased with his performance.

"Winston," Denise wailed. "Why did you tell her you'd give me a message? You should have said I've left the country or something!"

"I said I'd give you a *massage!*" Winston grinned. "And I will. Anytime."

"Seriously, Winston, why did you say you would pass on this woman's number?"

"Fear of authority?" Winston joked. "Inability to resist a woman's plea?"

"What about *my* plea!" Denise snapped. "I guess you think this is funny. Well, it's easy for you to laugh. You're not the one they're after!"

Winston leaned over and kissed Denise on the cheek, but she turned her head. Sighing, Winston rolled onto his back, trying to think of a way to cheer her up. Obviously making jokes wasn't helping. "Don't worry, sweetheart," he said. "Remember, this is America. We don't have debtors' prisons here."

"And remember, this is SVU," Denise replied. "A pretty expensive school. My bad credit is already jeopardizing my student loans, and without loans I won't be able to afford college!"

Yikes! Winston hadn't considered *that* possibility! Glumly he stared at the ceiling. They *had* to come up with a plan, pronto.

Denise felt her stomach begin to knot up again. The last few days she'd had serious stomach pains from worrying. Surely there was some way out of this situation, a loophole, a solution she'd missed that was actually right in front of her nose?

Not likely, Denise admitted miserably. *If only some ancient, childless relative I never met would kick the bucket and leave me a fortune!* But that wasn't going to happen. And short of a random burst of luck, Denise simply couldn't see an end to her financial woes. She'd been through each and every option painstakingly, but nothing looked promising.

"I need a quick, lucrative job," she said to Winston. "Something I can really sink my teeth into that would give me a nice big amount up front. If I could just get started with a decent-size payment, I'm sure those collection people would get off my back!"

"Maybe you could get a waitressing job," Winston ventured. "I saw a Help Wanted sign at the Red Lion Café yesterday."

Denise shook her head. "Nope. Even with decent tips a job like that won't cut it. From what I've heard, the Red Lion pays dirt for serious hours, and I can't do that with my class load. Plus it would probably take at least two weeks to get paid. That's time I just don't have!" She sighed and slurped unhappily on the dregs of her soda. "It's no use, Winnie. I'm going down."

The phone rang again, and Denise gestured to Winston to get it. It was probably the collection agent again. *Doesn't she have a life?* Denise thought gloomily. *Well, either way she* won't *get to speak to me!*

Winston grabbed the receiver. "Hello? Oh, hi, Jess!"

Denise breathed a sigh of relief. Jessica! A

happy surprise. Brightening, Denise took the phone from Winston. *Maybe she'll give me the scoop on her argument with Elizabeth,* she thought.

"Hey, girl," Denise sang into the phone, pleased at the distracting stream of babble that issued forth from the other side. Good old Jessica—she always managed to keep afloat, no matter what. Denise felt glad for the idle chatter. It was definitely welcome relief from contemplating her sorry fate.

"So I'm going to throw a gigantic party for Liz," Jessica announced enthusiastically. "But we have to act fast because I want to have it this Friday night at Theta house. It's a perfect time for it because there are no functions planned this weekend, so we get the run of the place—"

"Whoa! Wait up, Jess," Denise interjected. "I thought you and Liz had a big blowup today. And now you're throwing her a party? Back up a second!"

"Oh, that was nothing," Jessica said breezily. "Now, what do you think of the party idea? I've already got Lila, Isabella, and Alex committed to helping out, and now I want to enlist you."

"Whatever you need. Count me in!" Denise smiled, happy to be included in the plans for Elizabeth's party. She liked Elizabeth, and though she would be sad to see her leave, she was excited for her.

"Well," Jessica continued, "I'm sure my parents

will be only too happy to foot the bill, so I'm going to go all out on food and decorations. I'm thinking we could go for some kind of theme . . . or maybe not," she amended. "I mean, this is kind of like a good-bye party, so that might not work. Anyway, I'm going to make Theta house look incredible. Now all I need is to find someone to cater the party—I want the best food imaginable. Lila's taking care of the music, so that's one thing out of my hair. . . ."

As Jessica chattered on, Denise's mind began to tick. Jessica said she needed a caterer. And she also said that Mr. and Mrs. Wakefield would foot the bill! A slow smile spread across Denise's face. *Bingo!* she thought. A perfect opportunity had just landed in her lap—a way to end her financial troubles and at the same time help out a couple of women she cared about.

I *could do the catering!* Denise realized. She knew she could handle it—she'd always been a good cook, thanks to her dad, who was something of a gourmet chef. Now all she had to do was convince Jessica.

"I know how I can help," Denise began slowly. "Winston and I could do the catering. And at half the cost of a real caterer. What do you say, Jess? I know I can do it."

Denise held her breath in anticipation of Jessica's response. *Please say yes,* she begged silently.

"Brilliant idea, Denise! I can't believe I didn't think of it before! You're an excellent cook."

"So you really think your parents will cover the bill?"

"Definitely!" Jessica replied. "They're really proud of Liz. Then it's a deal. I know that the grub will be in capable hands."

"I assure you, it will be nothing short of a feast fit for a king—or a queen in this case."

"Awesome! So I'll leave it up to you, then. I can't wait," she added. "After this party there won't be a lobster left in Sweet Valley Bay. I'll check in with you later to discuss details. Until then, think food and think fancy—as long as it has a French name, I'm all for it. Canapés, crepes, croutons, escargot—you name it, we can pay for it!"

"Escargot!" Denise laughed and made a face. "You sure you want garden snails on the menu?"

"As long as they're expensive!" Jessica quipped. "Gotta go!"

After she hung up with Jessica, Denise turned to Winston excitedly. "Did you hear that? All my problems are solved!"

"And mine are only just beginning," Winston teased. "Me? A caterer? That'll be the day. I'm better at consuming than creating."

"Oh, don't worry. You won't have to do a thing . . . but follow my orders."

"Nothing new!" Winston joked. Denise faked a punch, laughing as Winston rolled to the floor dramatically.

This'll be a cinch, she thought happily. *I'll get to make some money fast, we'll do a great job, and everyone will hire us after they taste our mouth-watering creations. It's a long-term solution to paying off my debts . . . and an absolute miracle!*

Chapter
Seven

You're in a coma. Snap out of it! Elizabeth told herself as she poured herself another cup of coffee. It was already ten on a sunny Wednesday morning and still she wasn't awake. Yawning, she rubbed her eyes. This wasn't like her. Elizabeth was an early riser; even on weekends she had trouble sleeping in—something that had always annoyed Jessica.

If Jessica had it her way, she thought with a smile, *the world would rise at noon and stay up all night!*

Stifling another yawn, Elizabeth took a long gulp of her coffee. Although she'd fallen into bed pretty early the night before, she hadn't managed to sleep too well. Strange dreams kept her tossing and turning. In one she saw herself on a chairlift, somewhere in the Rocky Mountains. As her chair went up, a snowstorm began, and in the dream she became very anxious. On the other side of the lift pole, chairs were going down the slope to the warmth and safety of the cabins below. In the first chair were Nick and Jessica; in the second, Tom and Dana. They were laughing and having fun while Elizabeth, cold and alone, passed by. She called out to both couples, but no one seemed to notice; they soon vanished into the white of the blizzard.

Elizabeth shivered, recalling the dream. For a moment she considered what it might mean, then she put down her cup in irritation and went to get ready for the day. *Stop focusing on negative things,* she told herself. *Who cares what it means? It was just a stupid dream. It doesn't mean anything.*

But as she walked down the halls of SVU, Elizabeth couldn't help feeling wistful. All the friendly, familiar faces and the beautiful brick buildings with their leafy courtyards would soon be replaced by something unknown. Different people, different buildings, *different life.*

Elizabeth stopped to linger in front of the MacKellar fountain outside the administration building. This was one of her favorite places on campus, and as she rested her eyes on the beautiful white marble bathed in sunlight, the water glinting as it tumbled, she closed her eyes, trying to fix the image like a photograph in her mind. *So I can remember it when I'm gone,* she thought sadly.

After a moment Elizabeth took a deep breath and headed for the registrar's office, forcing herself to quell her feelings of sadness, concentrating instead on imagining her new school. She had seen pictures of it, and she had to admit, it looked like a beautiful campus. All glass and gleaming chrome, it was certainly very different from SVU, but by no means did that make it less appealing.

Plus Elizabeth knew the courses she would be taking would certainly be a step up from the journalism program at SVU. The Denver program boasted a state-of-the-art broadcast department, fully equipped with all the latest in digital technology. On top of that the professors were the very best, many of them Pulitzer Prize winners. *You're going to be in your element, Elizabeth,* she told herself, and walked through the double doors.

"May I help you?" the woman behind the desk inquired.

"I've come to cancel my classes for next semester," Elizabeth began, smiling at the kindly, bespectacled administrator. "I'm transferring."

"Your name, please?"

"Elizabeth Wakefield."

"Oh." Momentarily the woman frowned, then she smiled and looked up at Elizabeth. "Well, your friend just saved you the hassle."

"Excuse me?" Elizabeth replied, a puzzled look on her face.

"You just missed him. Your friend—Steve, is it? He just canceled your classes for you."

"*Steve?*"

"Or maybe . . . Scott? Yes, I think it was Scott. Forgive me, dear, my memory isn't what it should be."

"Scott!" Elizabeth blurted in surprise.

"Yes, it *was* Scott. A very nice young man too. He told me you'd be leaving, and together we went through your file and crossed your name off the class lists. So you're all set, dear."

"Uh, thanks," Elizabeth mumbled, and walked out of the building. The sun blinded her, and she shielded her eyes, frowning. *Just who does Scott think he is? My alter ego?* Elizabeth wondered as she walked briskly, anger mounting with each step. How dare Scott be so presumptuous! What he did was a downright invasion of privacy! *It's not as if I don't have legs,* she fumed. *I'm perfectly capable of doing my own paperwork!*

As she neared the path to Dickenson, Elizabeth caught sight of Scott's blond head bobbing above the crowd. Spinning on her heel, she changed direction and marched after him. "Scott!"

He turned and greeted her with a broad smile. "Oh, hi, Liz. I was just—"

"You were just . . . what? Rearranging my life?" Elizabeth snapped.

Scott looked bewildered. "I was going to say I was just thinking about you," he finished. "Why are you attacking me?"

"Because I don't appreciate your nosing around in my business!" Elizabeth retorted, her voice rising. "Why did you cancel my classes? I didn't ask you to!"

"Hey, hey," Scott interjected, holding up his hands in defense. "Calm down, Liz. I just thought I'd do you a favor! I figured you'd be pleased that you didn't have to deal with another tedious administrative chore. I was only trying to help, OK? I'm sorry if I offended you."

Elizabeth took a deep breath and put a hand to her forehead. *Get a grip*, she scolded herself as she felt her cheeks turn cherry red with shame and embarrassment. "I'm sorry, Scott." Her voice was low and trembling.

"Why are you so touchy?" Scott asked. "What's the matter?"

"Nothing." Elizabeth smiled weakly. "I'm just a little cranky, I guess. I haven't been getting much sleep lately. I'm sorry I took it out on you. I get really uptight when I'm overtired."

"That's OK. I understand." Scott smiled sympathetically and put his arm around Elizabeth's shoulders. "I know this moving stuff is stressful," he added. "Let's go get some coffee at the student union."

Elizabeth smiled back gratefully as he led her on a shortcut through the administration building. Scott was being so understanding. Yet somehow this made her feel worse, even a little alienated from him. Robotically she walked alongside Scott, her mind drifting as he made small talk. *He's so kind,* she thought, *but right now I can't relate—and I certainly can't relax!*

As they passed through the hallway a door opened and Professor Connor, one of Elizabeth's former lit teachers, stepped out of the dean's office, his eyes twinkling as he caught sight of Elizabeth. "Congratulations, Elizabeth!" he said with enthusiasm, and reached out to shake her hand. "I've just heard the news. I think it's marvelous."

"Thank you, Professor," Elizabeth replied, trying her best to look cheerful.

"Way to go, Liz!" another voice chimed in. It was Elsa Sheraton, a history TA whom Elizabeth had always admired. "I always knew you'd be going places. I'm only sorry we're going to lose you!"

"Yes . . . thank you," Elizabeth mumbled, breathing a sigh of relief when they finally moved on down the hall. *Peace and quiet,* Elizabeth thought longingly, looking forward to slumping into a booth in the student union.

"Elizabeth Wakefield!" a deep voice boomed as a door swung open. "Congratulations, young lady!" It was Professor Bloom, a portly, flamboyant humanities professor whose classes Elizabeth had always enjoyed. "You're headed for the top!" he continued, shaking his fist in the air. "Go get 'em!"

"Thank you." Again Elizabeth was touched, but

all the attention was making her claustrophobic. She felt her palms grow clammy and was relieved when Scott finally steered her through the doors of the student union cafeteria. But the sea of faces inside only furthered her anxiety, and she found herself hesitating to go in. *What's the matter with me?* Elizabeth thought. *Why am I panicking like this?*

Maybe because you might be making the biggest mistake of your life, a voice from deep inside answered. Shrugging off this thought angrily, she got her coffee, sat down, and began a conversation with Scott. But no matter how hard she tried, she knew she wouldn't be able to rid herself of the doubts she felt.

But I'm trapped now, she thought helplessly as she looked from Scott's crystalline blue eyes to the faces around her. Happy, laughing, carefree faces that seemed to belong to another person's life. Nothing felt real anymore.

"Jill Lombard, Melanie O'Neill, Bruce, Alex, Noah . . . that's it!" Jessica finished reeling off names to Denise and looked up, biting the end of her pen. "Did I forget anyone?"

"I don't think that's possible," Denise replied. "It looks like the entire student body is on this guest list."

"And it should be." Jessica smiled happily. "We're going all out, you know. It'll be the bash of the century."

"But don't you think we should cut some of those names off the list?" Denise suggested, a crease of worry on her brow. "I mean, come on, Jess, half these people have never even met Elizabeth, and we've got a budget to work with here. And who's *Georges Duchamp*, for goodness sake?"

"Cute French guy," Jessica replied. "He'll add much needed, um, *aesthetic* value next to Liz's homely library crew."

"But Jessica, the list is huge!" Denise wailed in exasperation.

Jessica waved away Denise's complaint with a perfectly manicured hand. "Denise," she began with exaggerated patience, "a party is *not* a party unless it's jam-packed. The more the merrier! Trust me, social events are my field of expertise."

"But—"

"No buts. This is not up for negotiation. We are having a major—make that *humongous*—glamfest for Liz. This will be the most talked about party in SVU history." Jessica sighed, a dreamy smile playing at her lips. She could see herself ushering everyone in, clad in her stunning new navy dress, her long legs accentuated by the stacked-heel shoes she'd just bought. She would be charming and witty—the perfect host. And people would be amazed at the incredible food and sophisticated decorations. They would assume she had done everything herself. *Of course, it wouldn't be necessary to burst the bubble,* Jessica thought. *I'll take the credit, no one will get hurt, and people will think I'm even more accomplished than I already am! Perfect!*

"Helloooo." Denise waved the guest list in front of Jessica's face. "Calling all space cadets . . ."

"Sorry," Jessica murmured. "I was just thinking of all the tasks we still have ahead of us. Starting with the menu. To help us, I brought some copies of *Gourmet,* which is to food what *Vogue* is to fashion." Jessica picked up a magazine and began leafing through it. "There's a special in here called 'Snacks for the Summer Soiree' that you have to see, Denise. It says, and I quote: 'No summer party is complete without succulent lobster. Grill them whole or serve pieces on crackers, but whatever you do, don't forget your crusty friend. And don't substitute if you want the very best, or live in fear of making a gastronomic faux pas!' "

Denise laughed. "That's ridiculous. Gastronomic faux pas. Please!"

Widening her eyes, Jessica looked up from the magazine. "Denise! This is *Gourmet* we're talking about—the watchdog of cuisine culture, guide to all the stars! There's even a recipe in here from Demi Moore."

"OK, Jess." Denise shrugged with a giggle. "You're the boss. Lobster it is!"

"And I think we should definitely serve asparagus. And different kinds of pâté . . ."

"You got it," Denise answered. "What about beluga caviar?"

"Mmmm. I like the sound of that. We should get . . . what? Five pounds?"

Laughing, Denise gathered her things and walked to the door of Jessica's room. "I was only kidding, Jess. One tiny teaspoon of beluga costs about as much as a semester's tuition! Anyway, I have to run. We'll talk later."

As the door closed behind Denise, Jessica felt very pleased with herself. The party plans were coasting along very smoothly indeed, and by Friday she would be throwing a party that would make the likes of Ivana Trump green with envy. Plus Elizabeth would be overwhelmed with all the trouble Jessica had taken. An added perk!

The ringing phone jolted Jessica from her musings, and she leaped to answer it, hoping it was Lila with details about the DJ.

"Hello, may I please speak to Elizabeth Wakefield?"

"Not in! May I take a message?" Jessica asked, and tuned out again, her mind flipping back to the party.

"This is Jerome Jefferies calling."

"OK, I'll tell her you called," Jessica replied hastily, eager to get the guy off the phone so she could make more party-related calls.

"Could you tell her I'll be in town on Friday and would like to meet with her?"

Now Jessica was intrigued. Who was this mystery man who wanted to see Elizabeth? "Do I know you?" she broke in.

"I don't think so," the man on the other end replied, chuckling. "I'm a representative from DCIR, and I thought since I'd be on the SVU campus this week, it would be nice to meet your roommate. May I leave my number?"

Jessica snapped to attention. This could be interesting. *Very* interesting. "Certainly." She took down the number and hung up slowly, her mind buzzing. *I shouldn't even be thinking this, but . . . if there's a man from DCIR wanting to meet Elizabeth . . .*

Could there be a way to keep Elizabeth from leaving without her knowing about it?

Don't! A warning bell sounded in the back of Jessica's brain, but it was as faint as the distant chirp of a cricket in a jungle next to the foghorn blare of Jessica's scheming mind. *It's a long shot, but it just might work!* she thought, reaching for the phone.

"Jerome Jefferies," the voice on the other end answered.

Taking a deep breath and gripping the phone, Jessica couldn't help smiling. "Hello," she began. "This is Elizabeth Wakefield. I'm returning your call. . . ."

"'You're invited,'" Tom read aloud, "'to the bash of the year. Join us for Elizabeth Wakefield's

119

big blastoff. . . .'" Tom frowned and tossed the invitation onto his desk. It had been lying there along with other internal campus mail when he'd walked into the WSVU newsroom.

Who sent it? he wondered. *And why?* Surely the whole world knew that he and Elizabeth were far from friends. *She* certainly wouldn't want him at her party. *And why should I go?* he thought angrily. *She'll just be flaunting herself with that jerk Scott the big shot. She'll totally rub my face in it!*

"Hey, Tom!" Tom looked up to see Dana saunter in. She looked ravishing as usual in a funky embroidered pumpkin-colored top and impossibly short sky blue skirt, her slender arms shimmering with silver bracelets. She smiled at him seductively and put her arms around his neck. "Say hi," she demanded, puckering her dark-lipsticked mouth for a kiss, her hazel eyes twinkling playfully.

"Hi," he murmured in response, and gave her a brisk, quick peck on the cheek. Looking her over, Tom knew he was crazy not to take advantage of Dana's adoration. What man wouldn't want to give her a passionate kiss right now? She was gorgeous and talented and a thousand other things, but Tom couldn't help it: He just wasn't in Dana mode.

Ever since he'd heard that Elizabeth was leaving, he'd been consumed with thoughts of her. Memories, regrets, anger, hurt. Every emotion in the book had seized him these past few days, and the common denominator was Elizabeth. With her on his mind Tom simply didn't have the room or the energy to focus on Dana. Luckily she didn't seem to notice that he was preoccupied.

"I'm having a great day," she announced. "Althea Johnstone canceled her daughter's lesson, so I have a full hour of free time." She winked. "If you know what I mean . . ."

"Uh, sorry, Dana, but I can't say the same," Tom replied, gently removing Dana's arms from his neck. "I've got a full load here." He gestured pointedly toward his desk.

"Hmmm." Dana's gaze fell on the invitation. "I can see that," she continued as she scanned the card. "Invitations to parties! We haven't had too many lately. Well, this ought to be fun." She tapped the card with a long, slender finger. "I'm in the mood for a party. 'The bash of the year,'" she read. "Of *course* we have to be there!"

"Well," Tom began, about to tell Dana that he had no intention of attending. Then he stopped. *What the heck! Why look like I'm pining?* With a small smile of satisfaction Tom looked Dana over appreciatively. *If I show up with this bombshell, it'll really ruffle Elizabeth's feathers.*

"Well . . . what?" Dana pouted. "You don't seem too excited."

"Well . . ." Tom smiled and placed his hands on Dana's waist. "Do you want to go with me?"

Dana raised an eyebrow. "What do you think? Of *course* I do!"

"Then let's go."

"Great!" Dana leaned into Tom and looked up at him coyly from under her long lashes. "We can finally spend some quality time together. We haven't seen much of each other lately, have we? What with all the newsroom work you've been doing. Even weekends!"

"I'm sorry, sweetheart," Tom replied, kissing the top of Dana's head. "It has been a little crazy around here."

"If you like crazy, I can show you crazy," Dana murmured, wrapping her arms tightly around Tom's waist.

"I like crazy," Tom replied, planting a kiss on Dana's full lips. *Take that, Elizabeth!* he thought as Dana kissed him back passionately. *I'll show up on Friday looking like the happiest man in the world, and you'll get a taste of your own medicine!*

Dana lingered over Tom's kiss, thrilled by his response to her suggestion they go to Elizabeth's party. Of course she *never* expected he'd want to hit that shindig, his being so touchy about Elizabeth and all. But a casual suggestion never did any harm, and besides, Dana *was* in the mood for a party. Any party. Even a Wakefield party.

I never thought he'd say yes, though, Dana thought with delight. *It must mean he's really over her after all!* She sighed with satisfaction and tightened her arms around Tom. She couldn't wait to walk into the party with Tom on her arm. She couldn't wait to see the look on prissy Miss Elizabeth's face. It would definitely be a moment of triumph.

And well earned, Dana thought, *after the runaround Tom has given me!* Mentally she flipped back through the many moments of doubt she'd had and all the schemes she'd had to concoct to keep Tom away from Elizabeth. Not that she ever understood what the attraction was anyway. *Elizabeth's not bad looking*, she admitted, *but she's so stuck-up. Besides, let's face it—I'm not exactly impaired in the looks department myself!* People had praised her looks and her musical abilities her whole life. They were her two main assets. *And I capitalize on them any way I can*, she thought as she smiled coquettishly at Tom.

"So, sweetheart," she purred. "What do you say? Why don't you take a breather from the world of reportage. . . ."

Tom grinned, and Dana couldn't help being struck by how sexy he was, with his gorgeous body and adorable smile. She had fallen for him so hard, right off the bat, and she knew she would do anything possible to keep him. She'd fight tooth and nail should there be any further Elizabeth-related incidents. Although perhaps now that wouldn't be necessary. Tom clearly wanted to go to the party with her, and Elizabeth had her own guy now . . . didn't she?

For a moment Dana recalled her odd conversation with Scott. She still hadn't figured it out. *Well, maybe he's just a weirdo!* she reasoned. *If something's up, I'll be ready for it.*

"I'm ready for a break," Tom murmured, grazing Dana's ear with his lips. Dana felt a shiver of desire ripple through her like an electric current. It was incredible—just being in Tom's arms was enough to send her up to cloud nine. "Let's get comfortable," Tom continued, scooping Dana up into his arms.

Tossing back her hair with a shriek of laughter, Dana clung to Tom as he moved toward the ratty old couch in the corner. *He is crazy about me!* she thought happily as he gently put her down. *And why shouldn't he be?* Dana reflected on all the guys she'd dated in the past. She'd had all of them eating out of her hand in no time. All except Tom. Which was probably why she liked him so much. He was a challenge, and Dana *loved* challenges.

"Give me a kiss," she demanded as Tom sat beside her.

"OK," Tom replied, kissing her so forcefully that Dana half fell off the couch.

"Mmmm. *Someone's* enthusiastic!" As Dana sat up, a cloud of dust rose off the couch. "Ugh," she moaned, brushing fibers off her shirt. "This thing is ready for the junkyard," she added, surveying the worn couch. It was a dark, ugly green, it sagged in the middle, and the upholstery was frayed and peeling back. "I think it's time WSVU sprang for a new couch. Really, this old thing needs to be retired."

"It's not that bad," Tom replied, a funny look on his face. He looked away, and Dana sensed rather than felt him shifting away from her.

Uh-oh, she thought. *Problem.* She knew Tom well enough to see when something was up. He had spoken in an offhand way, but Dana could see that he was preoccupied, no longer at ease. *And all because I told him to throw out a couch?* No, that seemed ridiculous. Tom wouldn't get testy over that. Dana pondered the possible reasons behind Tom's mood swing, eventually coming to a conclusion she didn't like one little bit. In her experience there was only one reason.

Elizabeth Wakefield.

"So what's the story behind this old thing anyway?" Dana asked, taking care to ensure a tone of voice that was somewhere between casual and knowing to cover all her bases. If there was some sentimental link between Elizabeth and the couch, she wanted Tom to know she suspected it. If not, she didn't want to make him think she was unfairly suspicious. *I've got to stay one step ahead of him,* she thought shrewdly. Mentally Dana psyched herself up for yet another possible "Elizabeth problem." If her suspicions were confirmed, she would be more than disappointed to discover that Tom still hadn't gotten the ice queen completely out of his system, but she would deal with it. She had no other choice.

Something flickered over Tom's face, and he cleared his throat. *OK*, Dana thought grimly, *here it comes! He'll come up with some lame thing about the couch, then say he has a lot of work, and would I mind if we didn't go to the party after all?*

"There's no story behind it," Tom replied. "I'm just . . . very attached to it because it's been here for so long."

He smiled at Dana, and she felt her spirits lift. Maybe she was imagining things. Maybe there was no problem after all. Looking over at Tom now, Dana found herself wondering if she was just being paranoid. He seemed totally relaxed.

"I've been reluctant to let it go," Tom continued, patting the arm of the couch, "because . . . it has character." He pulled a thread from the fabric of the arm. "But you're right; it's time to let it go. Sometimes you have to get rid of the old and bring in the new."

"I couldn't agree with you more," Dana replied delightedly. Clearly progress *was* being made. It was good to see that all her hard work was finally paying off, even if it would still take a while for her to really relax and truly believe that Tom was over Elizabeth. Dana was still a little wary despite Tom's attitude. She *had* to be wary. She didn't want to be caught off guard. And until Elizabeth was safely dispatched to her new home,

Dana knew she had to continue to be on the look-out for trouble. *Don't get lulled into a false sense of security!* she cautioned herself.

"But before I throw out this couch," Tom continued with a mischievous smile, breaking into Dana's thoughts, "I want to get some use out of it."

As Tom pulled her down with him Dana closed her eyes in delicious anticipation of his next kiss. *But be careful,* she warned herself. *People can still get robbed in broad daylight!*

Chapter
Eight

"It's almost ten, and you're not dressed yet?" Elizabeth asked as she grabbed her leather backpack and quickly knotted her hair into a ponytail. "Jess, Friday is still a weekday, you know!"

"I, uh, only have class at eleven," Jessica answered a little guiltily, hoping Elizabeth wouldn't suspect anything. "I'm just so *tired*," she added, throwing in a yawn and rubbing her eyes. It was a beautiful warm morning, and sunlight streamed in through the window of room 28. Jessica had been awake for two hours already, plotting and planning. But it wasn't easy to keep things hidden from her sister.

"Even for you this is late," Elizabeth replied, laughing. "Tell you what: I'll lighten your load by skipping the shopping spree this afternoon. I know you'll have lots of last minute party stuff to do. I'll bet that's why you're so tired. All this organizing and running around."

Good. She's buying it, Jessica thought. *Now leave, Liz. Leave!*

"So . . . I'll see you later, then?" Jessica pulled back her covers and gave an exaggerated yawn. "You'd better hustle, or you're going to be late for class."

"I thought *I* was supposed to say that to *you*," Elizabeth remarked, fidgeting. "But . . . well . . . I just wanted to talk to you for a sec."

Uh-oh. Is she on to me? A flash of panic bolted through Jessica's stomach. Did she figure out her plan? Maybe she'd found out somehow. . . .

"I just wanted to say," Elizabeth began, twisting her hands, "that I really appreciate what you're doing for me."

"Huh?" Jessica frowned. "Um . . . l-like what?" she asked guiltily, praying Elizabeth wasn't about to nail her into her coffin.

"The party tonight. All the support you're giving me. It means so much, Jess."

Elizabeth looked up at Jessica with gratitude, and Jessica felt another wave of guilt wash over her. Luckily it only lasted a minute and was soon replaced by a more urgent wave of panic. *Great timing, Liz,* Jessica thought in desperation. *I have to be out of here in ten minutes, and you have to pick now to have a tender moment!*

"Well, you deserve nothing but the best!" Jessica answered brightly. *Now do me a favor and get out of here!*

"I just want to be sure you know how much

130

this means to me," Elizabeth went on.

"I know, don't worry," Jessica reassured her. She got out of bed and began pacing near the door. *Maybe I can get her to leave by the power of suggestion,* she reasoned.

But Elizabeth stayed where she was, searching, it seemed, for more words. Jessica had to take action. "Liz, I appreciate what you're saying. You don't need to say another word." *Really! Not another word!* Jessica prayed, ushering Elizabeth toward the door. "Now you just get moving and don't give it another thought! I don't want you to be late on my account. Go on!"

Finally! Jessica slammed the door behind Elizabeth and sped toward her closet, shedding her pajamas as she went. There wasn't even time to shower! Pulling out a tight red Lycra micromini that she had worn to a *Rocky Horror Picture Show* party and an unworn gold lamé shirt that Lila had somehow convinced her to buy, Jessica began to get ready.

She grabbed a hairbrush and teased her silky hair. Then she slapped on some garish eye makeup and blusher, topping it off by skimming an obnoxiously red lipstick across her lips. After pulling on her spikiest pair of stilettos Jessica surveyed herself in her full-length mirror. She looked somewhere between cheap and just plain ridiculous. *Perfect!*

Grabbing a huge pair of sixties sunglasses and pulling on a long trench coat to disguise herself,

Jessica dashed out of room 28 and down the hall. As she neared the journalism building, where she'd agreed to meet Jerome Jefferies, she slowed down and took off her coat and glasses. Her toes pinched, and her ankles ached. Most of all, she felt a sharp splinter of guilt pierce her insides. But it went away almost as fast as it had appeared. *I have to be sneaky,* Jessica assured herself. *It's not like I want to be, but I have to stop Liz from leaving. This is for her own good!*

Reaching room 54, she took a deep breath before knocking.

"Come in," came the reply, and Jessica opened the door to find herself face-to-face with a nice-looking man seated at the desk.

"Jerome Jefferies?" she asked, lowering her voice seductively.

"Yes." The man smiled at her, giving nothing away. *He must notice my awful outfit,* Jessica thought with satisfaction. *He's horrified, but he's just too polite to show it.*

Jerome Jefferies stood up and extended his hand. "Pleased you could make it, Elizabeth," he said, looking into Jessica's eyes.

"Grab me another pile of those portobello mushrooms, would you, Winnie?" Denise dumped an armload of focaccia into her already overloaded shopping cart. She stopped to check off the items on her list that she already had and then swung the cart around to the next aisle.

"Trust me to get the cart with the poltergeist wheel," she groaned as she tried to maneuver the cart one way and it turned the other.

"Denise," Winston began, giving the cart a hefty push. "May I remind you that you've already spent more money on the groceries than we actually have in the budget Jessica gave us."

Denise flipped her hair out of her eyes and tossed several cans of smoked oysters into her cart. "Winston, the first rule about moneymaking is, You have to *spend* money to *make* money."

"And you would know," Winston retorted sarcastically.

"Look." Denise sighed, rolling her eyes. "This is an investment. If we go all out for this party, we'll get tons more offers to cater events, and the cash will come rolling in. What goes around comes around."

"And what goes out of your pocket *stays* out of your pocket!" Winston muttered. "I mean, just yesterday you were desperate to come up with some cash, and now today you're buying smoked oysters we don't need." Winston took the cans from the cart and replaced them on the shelf. He gave Denise a puzzled look. "I don't understand you women. You really *are* from Venus."

Denise shrugged and pushed her cart forward. "I realized this morning that if I can work around my short-term needs, I'll be way better off in the long run. If we do a so-so job with a few carrot sticks, I can *maybe* pay off my minimum. But if we make a big splash, I'll be able to completely pay off my debt in no time! Don't you see?" She turned to Winston, who was eyeing the piled-up cart dubiously. "This is a golden opportunity. We just have to ride it out."

"I'll bet a lot of people have learned to regret those words in their time," Winston replied. "Let's see, how many famous people have gone bankrupt through debt? Well, there's—"

"Hush!" Denise snapped. "Have a little faith, Winnie. Honestly, you sound like my father!"

As they moved to the checkout counter Denise continued to plead her case to Winston. Deep down, however, she *was* a little worried. She knew she was taking a gamble, and she could only pray it would work. *But I have to seem ultraconfident to Winston,* she told herself, *or else he'll stop me from doing this!*

As she paid the extravagant bill Denise avoided meeting Winston's eyes. It *was* larger than she'd budgeted for. *But it will all be worth it,* Denise told herself as they headed for the fish store across the road.

"Anyway," Denise continued as they surveyed the rows of silvery seafood displayed in front of them, "that collections woman seems to have given up. She hasn't called me once today!"

"Don't speak too soon," Winston replied gloomily. "Those people are very slippery."

134

"So's this floor," Denise said, looking down warily. "It's probably full of slimy fish scales. Ugh, I *hate* fish!"

"Then what are we doing visiting our friends from the sea?" Winston asked, smiling at Denise's disgust-wrinkled face.

"We're not buying fish, we're buying lobster," Denise replied.

"Denise!" Winston groaned. "That's only *the* most expensive delicacy in Sweet Valley—or the world, I should say."

"I know." Denise smiled. "But it's going to be our grand coup, our masterpiece—"

"Our financial undoing," Winston added.

"Shut your trap," Denise said crossly. "And stop whining. I've prepared for this. It will be OK."

Winston held up his hands in defeat as Denise walked up to the counter, eyeing the large, succulent-looking lobsters crawling in the tank behind the counter.

"May I help you?" one man inquired.

Denise took a deep breath and ignored Winston's fidgeting. "Yes, you certainly may!"

As she pulled out a thick wad of Wakefield-supplied cash and waved it in the man's face, Denise smiled in satisfaction. "This is going to be great," she told Winston, who looked at her dubiously. "Great!" she repeated excitedly as he folded his arms in a huff.

I hope, she added silently.

*   *   *

"Mr. Jefferies," Jessica purred seductively as she clasped his outstretched hand. "It is *such* a pleasure to meet you."

"And you, Elizabeth," Jerome Jefferies replied, beaming. "But call me Jerome. I'm not *that* much older than you, you know."

"Well, you certainly don't look it," Jessica gushed, letting her eyes linger on the lanky, sandy-haired Denver rep. "I mean, you don't look a day over thirty-four!" she simpered.

Jerome let out a bellow of laughter. "Actually I only just turned thirty-one."

"Oh! Well, I'm *awfully* sorry, Jerome." She widened her blue-green eyes, which were heavily caked with black eyeliner and silver mascara. "I guess I'm not the brightest bulb in the chandelier!"

"Now, now, you're being awfully modest," Jerome answered with a smile. "I happen to have your Denver application right here," he added, tapping a manila folder. "And I must say, you're an extremely impressive young woman. Your academic record is excellent, your reporting portfolio is nothing short of brilliant, and aside from that you seem to have involved yourself in a variety of extracurricular and community-related activities."

"Oh, that's a little exaggerated!" Jessica replied, pointing at the folder, but Jerome continued to beam at her. *Darn it, Liz,* Jessica thought in annoyance. *Did you* have *to chair that stupid poetry club? Did you* have *to volunteer for Literacy*

Now? Did you have *to offer your services to Gardening for Seniors?* Elizabeth truly *was* perfect. It was disgusting! Jessica knew she'd have to work extra hard to convince Jerome that Elizabeth was no saint.

Moistening her lips, Jessica fluttered her eyelashes bashfully and walked over to the window so that Jerome could get the full effect of her skimpy outfit. "Isn't it a marvelous day?" she asked, leaning slightly out the window. "This is *not* a day for study, is it?" She flashed Jerome her most dangerous smile.

But Jerome didn't bat an eyelash. "Absolutely not," he replied. "It's a day for being outdoors and enjoying nature. And if there's one thing we can offer you in Colorado, Elizabeth, it's nature!" He opened his briefcase. "I'm sure you'll miss Sweet Valley, but you'll forget all about it when you're in the beautiful Rocky Mountains." Smiling, he withdrew a glossy brochure. "I've brought you the latest school bulletin. It's hot off the presses and contains some extra information on the recreational activities we have to offer. Do you like skiing?"

Jessica gagged as if she were coughing up a hair ball. "Puh-*leeze!* I *hate* skiing! It's a sport for . . . for . . . for people who aren't good at any other sports!" She waited for Jerome to react, but his face remained cheerful. *If he doesn't stop smiling, he's going to crack his face,* Jessica thought in irritation.

Suddenly she began to wonder if Jerome was simply "not all there." *The poor man must be paddling with one oar,* Jessica mused, wondering what she could pull as her next move.

"Well, skiing isn't all we have," Jerome continued. "There's biking, hiking, fishing, river rafting . . . you name it!"

"Is there a beach?" Jessica asked, opening her eyes wide. "I love lying out!" *A beach in Colorado?* she asked herself, stifling a giggle. *Duh! Now he'll be* convinced *that they made a mistake by accepting Liz. No one could be that ignorant—not even me!*

"Oh, Elizabeth, you sure are funny." Jerome chuckled. "I like that! It's refreshing to meet a serious young journalist who still has a sense of fun. Too many of your kind take the weight of the world on their shoulders," he added. "And I must say, I find many of the students I meet somewhat false. They're so busy trying to impress that they don't realize they're coming on too strong!"

If this *isn't coming on too strong,* Jessica thought, looking down at the low neck of her gold lamé blouse, *then I don't know what is!*

"Well . . . I'm glad you approve of me," she purred, settling on the window ledge and extending her long, stilettoed legs.

"Not only me, Elizabeth. The DCIR faculty approves of you as a whole." Jerome clasped his hands in a confidential gesture. "We're just so *thrilled* that you're coming to us to hone your talents. We want to help you blossom and grow as a journalist."

Blossom and grow? Oh, puke! Jessica could barely stomach *looking* at this annoying man, much less listening to the sickly sweet words coming out of his mouth. The whole scene was putrid. *Think, Jessica!* she ordered herself. *Find a way to turn this guy off!*

Jessica pulled out a stick of gum and popped it into her mouth. *That alone ought to do it,* she thought with satisfaction. Then, affecting her most bored expression, she cracked her gum and gave Jerome a halfhearted smile. "I don't know, Jerome," she began. "I guess I'm just not the blossoming, growing type, if you know what I mean. I really just want to go to Denver to party. I heard the scene is pretty wild out there."

"Oh, you heard right," Jerome boomed. "Take it from one who knows! I'm a DCIR graduate myself." His eyes misted over. "Those days, those wild carefree days . . . Yes, Elizabeth, you *will* have a great time. But," he added, flashing her a big smile, "we'll still find time to shape you into the top journalist you're going to be, don't you worry."

Jessica's mouth fell open like a trapdoor. *This guy is made of reinforced concrete!* she thought remorsefully. *I couldn't just fail at making him think Elizabeth is a trashy airhead. No, I had to go and remind him of his golden olden college days! Way to go, genius!*

139

Jerome looked at his watch. "Well, Elizabeth, I'm extremely glad to have met you," he said, snapping his briefcase shut. "I would have loved to talk with you more, but I'm afraid I have to get going to a conference now."

Oh no! Jessica thought in desperation. She could only make one more move. She *had* to make this guy take a bad impression of her sister back to the Denver Center of Investigative Reporting. She *had* to stop Elizabeth from leaving Sweet Valley.

Standing up slowly, Jessica flashed another deadly, seductive Jessica Wakefield smile. She sashayed over to the man, moving her hips as much as was humanly possible in her unwieldy shoes. "Jerry," she cooed throatily. "It sure is a pity you have to go. I've truly enjoyed meeting you."

"And I you, Elizabeth," Jerome responded with a bright smile. "You certainly are charming. You'll be an asset to our program. Maybe you can loosen up the rest of the student body. Well, until then!"

Jessica shook Jerome's hand reluctantly. *Last chance,* a voice inside her said. *Do something!*

Puckering her scarlet lips, Jessica planted a big, smacking kiss on Jerome's cheek as she continued to pump his hand vigorously.

"Whoa!" Jerome exclaimed in surprise, his eyebrows shooting up into his hair.

Good one! Jessica congratulated herself. *Now for sure he'll think Liz is straight off her rocker!*

But Jerome merely rubbed his cheek and

laughed. "That's a bright color," he said. "Just like you, Elizabeth. You sure are a bright one. You'll make your mark, there's no doubt about that! Well, it certainly has been a pleasure," he added, and went to open the door.

Jessica's face burned bloodred with fury. *Is this wacko on loan from a mental institution?* she wondered. *Some journalist* he *must be!* She flounced out of the office without even bothering to give Jerome a backward glance, balling her coat in her hands with anger. What a disaster!

Muttering angrily to herself, Jessica shot down the steps of the building, ignoring the looks she was getting from other students. *Well done, Jessica,* she chided herself. *Not only did you* not *give a bad impression of Elizabeth, but you made things even worse—you made them love her even more!*

Tom scanned the row of books in front of him and then consulted the list in his hand. He already had *Madame Bovary, For Whom the Bell Tolls,* and *Portrait of the Artist as a Young Man.* Now all he needed was *The Sound and the Fury* to round out the books that still remained on his literary classics syllabus. Sighing, he took a book from the shelf and examined it. There was a day when book shopping would have been something he'd enjoyed. But that was back when he and Elizabeth were together. They had spent many hours in conversation about their favorite writers. And many hours in this very bookstore, drinking coffee in the reading café on the upper floor. *We would have made a day of it*, Tom thought sadly. *But those days are over now.*

Lost in thought, Tom gazed at the cover of the book in his hand without really registering it. *Get over it, Watts!* he demanded silently. In a matter of hours he would be attending Elizabeth's party with Dana, and he had to look as if he were the luckiest guy on earth.

It was going to be tough to pull off.

"Faulkner. Pretty highbrow." Tom looked up to see who was speaking and found himself face-to-face with none other than Scott Sinclair. Clenching his jaw, Tom willed himself not to react. But Scott's smug smile indicated he was obviously enjoying this little chance meeting.

"Some of us like to read," Tom replied coolly, turning his attention back to the book.

"And some of us don't!" Scott said. "I don't know, Watts, but I prefer the thrill of being out there on the beat to reading quietly on the sidelines. But then you probably know that already."

"Oh, sure," Tom replied smoothly without a hint of sarcasm in his voice. "The story you did with Elizabeth certainly proved it. You're the man, Sinclair. The rest of us can only hope to do as well as you do."

"Well," Scott answered with a smile. "I must say, it *is* good to be recognized for my achievements.

142

And before long I'll be starting the new semester in Denver with Elizabeth." Scott emphasized her name just enough to cause Tom to stiffen.

I ought to punch out that slimy jerk right now! Tom thought angrily, then controlled himself. Words could do the job just as well.

"It must feel good to be rewarded for all your hard work," Tom said, placing just the right amount of emphasis on the words *hard work*. "I mean, it's not as if you had any *connections* or anything. You did it all on your own, Sinclair. I gotta hand it to you."

Tom smiled, pleased with his retort. Scott's father was on the board of a huge conglomerate that not only controlled *NEWS2US* but also underwrote DCIR's undergrad program. Tom knew a clear case of nepotism when he saw it, and he had held nothing back in his feature story on WSVU. Elizabeth might not have bought it, but Tom knew it had gotten to Scott then, and it sure was getting to him right now. *Go ahead, Sinclair,* he thought with satisfaction. *Pretend you're not stung!*

Scott nodded thoughtfully for a moment and then turned to Tom with a smug, I-feel-sorry-for-you look. "You're a bad loser, Watts," he said. "You shouldn't show it. It's not flattering."

"And you're a false winner. You bend the rules to get what you want. I wouldn't call that fair game!" Tom shot back, unable to stop his voice from rising.

"Sounds like a jealous ex-boyfriend to me," Scott replied evenly.

Tom drew a sharp intake of breath, momentarily caught off balance. It was true. He would love to be in Scott's shoes right now, if only to be closer to Elizabeth. But still, Sinclair was slime, and Tom would rather spend his days plugging away anonymously at WSVU than being showered with offers and praise all because of a father in high places. He had pride. Scott didn't. Tom could only wonder how long it would take for Elizabeth to see just what a disgusting creep Sinclair was.

"I could never be jealous of you," Tom said, looking at Scott as if he were a reptile. "You're a lightweight and a fake, and one of these days Liz is going to find that out."

Smiling, Scott turned to leave. "You know something?" he asked lightly. "Liz was right about you." With that, Scott walked away, leaving Tom shaking with rage and confusion.

What did he mean, "Liz was right about you"? he wondered furiously. *Right about* me? *Right about* what?

Tom focused on the dizzying array of books on the shelves around him in the hopes of putting the incident out of his mind. But it didn't work. After a moment he walked over to the empty space near the information desk and leaned against the wall, closing his eyes. He had a blinding headache.

144

Liz was right about you.

Scott's infuriating last words raced through Tom's mind, echoing back and forth, making his head spin. He could go crazy wondering what that sentence meant. Was Scott just saying that to tick him off? Or had Elizabeth told Scott something . . . shocking? Disgraceful? Scandalous?

True?

Tom squeezed his eyes shut and massaged his throbbing temples. *What does Elizabeth really think of me?* he wondered. *And why do I care about it so much? Maybe tonight I'll finally find out.*

"How do you want these mushrooms chopped?" Winston asked Denise, turning to her with a large chopping knife in his hand. This cooking stuff was even more tedious than Winston had expected. They'd only been in the Theta kitchen for a couple of hours, they still had a ton to do, and already he was tired!

I sure am the perfect boyfriend, he thought. *Would Bruce do this for Lila? Would Nick do this for Jess? Nope, I don't think so!*

"I think they should be sliced thinly," Denise replied as she sautéed onions and peppers in a pan.

"What's your definition of thin?" Winston demanded.

"Like this." Denise took the knife from Winston, and in a few deft strokes a whole mushroom was reduced to paper-thin pieces.

"Wow," Winston breathed in admiration. "You make it look so easy."

"That's because I'm gifted!" Denise sang, smiling. "Now get moving, Winnie. Time is of the essence!"

"OK, OK." Winston sighed and grudgingly began to cut the mushrooms.

"Too thick!" Denise called out sharply moments later.

"Hey!" Winston replied. "I'm beginning to feel like Cinderella here. Anyway, there's nothing wrong with my cutting techniques. Look at this!" Proudly he held up what he perceived to be a neat sliver.

Denise studied it for two seconds. "It's a wedge."

"It is not! It's as thin as the skin of an onion!" Winston grinned as Denise rolled her eyes.

"On second thought," she stated matter-of-factly, "you're right. It's not a wedge . . . it's a *doorstop!*"

"That does it!" Winston bellowed. With a wild whoop he began chasing a shrieking Denise around the kitchen. Finally he caught her and pinned her up against the fridge. "Now take it back!" he demanded.

"No!" Denise giggled.

"Say it: 'Winston Egbert is a master chef, and I am but a lowly novice.'"

"I will not!"

"Then I shall have to tickle you!" Winston started tickling Denise until she begged for mercy and made him resume his chopping. Banging the knife down clumsily, Winston fantasized about the eating he would get to do later. Denise had prepared all sorts of delectable snacks, and Winston was going to make quite sure that he tasted each and every one of them.

"Winnie, sweetheart?" Denise called, breaking into Winston's reverie. "Will you bring me the lobsters? I've got my hands full."

"Sure thing, Your Highness," Winston replied, grabbing a miniquiche and stuffing it into his mouth quickly before Denise could see. "Where did you put them?" he added, staring into the fridge. "I can't see them."

"What do you mean, where did *I* put them," Denise retorted. "*I* didn't put them anywhere!" She looked worried, and then a knowing smile broke across her face. "Another one of your practical jokes?" she asked.

"No, I'm serious. Where are they?"

"I thought you brought them in!" Denise exclaimed, staring into the empty fridge.

"No! I thought *you* brought them in!" Winston replied, dread spreading through his insides.

"Then they must still be . . . *ohhh nooo!*" Denise wailed, dropping her spatula to the floor.

Chapter
Nine

I should have brought a wheelbarrow! Elizabeth thought, grimacing as she hoisted the heavy bag of books she was carrying up onto her shoulder. _Trust me to be overprepared for next semester, buying books long before I need them._ Now that she was going to Colorado, she had to trade in everything she'd bought. No sense in keeping books she wouldn't need for courses she wouldn't be taking. As she trudged toward the bookstore a familiar person stepped out and walked the other way, his back to her.

Tom.

Almost unconsciously Elizabeth made herself pass by the bookstore. Keeping a safe distance, she followed Tom as he headed across campus. She didn't even know why she was doing it, but it was as if her feet had a mind all their own. She walked, cheeks burning, her eyes fixed on his back. Despite all the distress he had caused her,

Elizabeth still couldn't help admiring his broad shoulders and tall, lean frame.

All of a sudden Tom stiffened and slowed down as if he sensed he was being watched. As he turned slowly his eyes met Elizabeth's, and she froze, rooted to the spot. His face darkened with anger, and for a moment they stared at each other in silence. Elizabeth felt herself begin to tremble, and adrenaline rushed through her body from the pure force of Tom's angry gaze. *But I won't back away,* she told herself, and with a deep breath she forced herself to walk forward.

Woodenly Elizabeth moved toward Tom and stopped only inches in front of him. She *had* to confront him. She *had* to try and make peace with him. Even if she failed again, she knew she still had to try. That way she would rest easier in the knowledge that she had done everything in her power to reach out to him before she left SVU forever.

"Tom . . . ," she began, her voice thick with emotion. "This is very hard for me."

"What is?" Tom's voice was cold and steady.

I can't stop now, Elizabeth told herself, in spite of her impulse to back away and run.

"This . . ." She struggled for words. "The way things are between us. I can't believe we're really enemies after the way it used to be. . . ." Elizabeth trailed off, her voice growing smaller. Twisting her hands, she looked down at the ground. *I wish I could just sink through the concrete,* she thought miserably. *Just fall away and disappear* . . .

Tom's expression changed. Had it softened? Had she finally broken through his stony exterior? Elizabeth couldn't tell. "Look, Elizabeth," he began in a low voice, but something—someone—cut him short.

"Hi there!" Dana stepped up between them, smiling widely, her voice hard and bright. She slipped her arm through Tom's possessively. "Oh, hi, Elizabeth. You look . . . nice."

Right! I'm wearing a sweatshirt and cutoffs, and she's in a hot pink minidress, red go-go boots, and a vintage shawl! Only Dana would wear something so unappealing and flashy. Elizabeth could barely stand to look at her.

Tom also looked uncomfortable and, Elizabeth was pleased to note, barely acknowledged Dana. But he regarded Elizabeth with impassive eyes too—the softness Elizabeth had thought she'd seen flickering in his face was definitely gone now.

"We're really looking forward to your party tonight," Dana gushed, looking at Elizabeth from under her long lashes. "Sounds like the perfect way to say good-bye," Dana continued. "Leaving with a big splash!"

I'd like to say good-bye to you, Elizabeth thought angrily. *Just who invited you anyway? And Tom too! Why would he even want to be there?*

Elizabeth felt a white-hot current of anger pulse through her as she watched Dana look her up and down mockingly, but she controlled herself, forcing a smile to her lips. She didn't want Dana to feel she'd gotten the upper hand. "Yes, isn't it great?" she replied calmly. "Jessica's throwing it for me. Anyway, I have to get going now."

"Well, we'll see you later," Dana sang out as Elizabeth trudged off.

How about not? Elizabeth fumed. That girl was sure to ruin her party. And Tom. Why couldn't he see how false, cloying, and clingy Dana really was?

Get ahold of yourself! Elizabeth thought. Tom wasn't worth getting this worked up over, and Dana . . . well, Dana was even less worth her worries.

You're just jealous, she told herself, and then instantly denied it. She sighed miserably. Everything was in a muddle. She didn't know whether she was coming or going anymore. And seeing Tom just threw her a curve every time.

Why? she asked herself. *Why does his opinion matter to you so much? Why can't you stop loving and hating him and just get on with your life already?*

There was no clear answer to that question. It had been haunting Elizabeth for days. She only hoped it wouldn't torture her forever.

"PU!" Denise shrieked, holding her nose and turning away from the smelly lobster meat that was lying in the trunk of Winston's famed orange

Volkswagen Bug. "How could we have been so dumb? These lobster's have been sitting here for hours!"

"That's a very expensive smell," Winston added, turning to Denise sympathetically. "I'm sorry, sweetheart. I could have sworn you'd brought them in."

"Darn it!" Denise lifted the bag gingerly and threw it to the ground. "What are we going to do now?" She groaned. "I have exactly twelve dollars and fifty-eight cents to my name. Not even enough for two lobsters, let alone a whole pile!"

Winston put his arm around Denise's shoulders. "It's no use crying over spilled milk," he said. "We'll just have to come up with a fallback plan."

"Yeah, well, I'm going to fall on my *face* when Jessica hears about this," Denise replied tearfully. "I'm all out of ideas, Winnie. We have four hours left before the guests arrive, and Jessica is counting on me to provide them with the best food this side of the equator! What are we gonna do?"

Winston sighed. Things were definitely not going their way. *Think, Egbert!* he ordered himself. But no matter how hard he tried, no magical solution appeared before him. Looking over at Denise's miserable face, he knew he'd *have* to come to the rescue. There was no doubt about it. He, Winston, would somehow have to save the day.

"Don't worry, Denise," Winston soothed, willing himself to sound positive. "I'll come up with something to replace the lobster. You just go back into the kitchen, and I'll go and sort this out." Winston gave his best, most confident smile and gently urged Denise to return to Theta house. "I'll take care of it," he added. "Honest."

After some prodding, Denise smiled wanly and headed back into the house. With a take-charge attitude Winston gunned the Bug's engine, pulled out into the street, and sped onto the highway, running through a list of possible lobster substitutes all the way. *Crab? Scallops? Jumbo shrimp?* he wondered. *Too expensive!* Heck, he couldn't even taste the difference between them to begin with. But that didn't matter. He had to come through for Denise because if he didn't, he could lose her forever.

His heart pounding painfully in his chest, Tom swallowed hard as he watched Elizabeth walk away. He ignored the pressure of Dana's arm on his and the stream of unimportant chatter that was issuing from her mouth.

Elizabeth's confrontation had come as a big surprise. Tom thought she was never going to speak to him again, that she truly didn't care what he thought of her. But her coming up and talking to him like that . . . that had to count for something, didn't it?

Elizabeth's words rang in Tom's ears. *"I can't believe we're really enemies after the way it used to be. . . ."* Tom couldn't believe it either. But on second thought, should he even believe Elizabeth's words now? After all, she'd rejected him and badmouthed him, and now she was leaving for another school with another man. And yet . . . she had seemed sincerely upset a few minutes back and appeared to want to put things right between them one way or another.

Tom was mystified. Which was it? Did Elizabeth care, or was she just fooling with him?

". . . so then I told her that if she thought she could take first chair from me, she had another thing coming. Then *she* actually said to *me,* 'I'm not playing second fiddle to you!' Can you believe that, Tom? Talk about your dumb puns . . ."

For a moment Tom was seized with anger. Who cared about Dana's stupid gossip? *Shows how little she really knows me,* Tom thought grimly. "Look, Dana," he interrupted. "I have a lot of stuff to take care of right now, so if you don't mind, I'll just get going and see you later."

"Uh, OK," Dana replied in a slightly hurt tone. "Later," she added more brightly, and after a moment's hesitation she turned and walked in the direction of the cafeteria.

Tom barely felt a twinge of remorse at the way he'd cut Dana off. And he hardly noticed her absence as he moved in the direction of the gym. He was too wrapped up in his thoughts of Elizabeth to notice anything or anyone around him. It was

155

all too mystifying . . . one moment Elizabeth was on, the next moment she was off, like a light switch.

Perhaps he would approach her at the party, pull her aside and demand the truth once and for all. Yes, *that* would work! Maybe he would hear the words he really wanted to hear. Words like "I'm not leaving" and "I still love you."

She must be thinking about me too, he thought, a tingle of hope and excitement shooting up through his body. He would have to take her aside at the party, there was no question about it. . . .

That's if you can get her away from Scott! Yeah, right. Knowing Scott, he'd be stuck to Elizabeth like a leech. *I'd have to pry him off her with a crowbar,* Tom thought in irritation. Scott was a sly one. He knew what was going on, and Tom knew Scott would do whatever it took to hang on to Elizabeth.

And who could blame him?

Tom stopped walking and ran his hands through his hair. Suddenly it was all too much. Elizabeth coming up to him, Scott badgering him, and tonight Elizabeth's good-bye party. *It's a* good-bye *party!* Tom told himself sternly. *That means good-bye! No matter what, Elizabeth is leaving. And maybe that's why she approached you—to make peace with you so she can be happy in her new life with that creep.*

The thought was so horrendous that it brought

tears to Tom's eyes. "I'm a fool." He groaned aloud. "I'm a jealous, misguided fool."

I drove the best thing that ever happened to me right into the arms of another man, he thought miserably, kicking a piece of asphalt in frustration. *And now it's too late. Soon Elizabeth will be gone. Forever.*

Jessica glanced in the window of Yvette's, a new and highly exclusive boutique in Sweet Valley. Eyeing a raw silk burgundy shift with matching sling-back pumps, Jessica forced herself to look away. What was the point? She didn't have enough money. *And you don't deserve anything now either,* she told herself. *After your lame performance with Jerome Jefferies, you ought to crawl into a hole and hide, not strut your stuff in front of the whole world!*

Scowling, Jessica marched past the boutique and dawdled in front of the next. A beautiful apricot-and-turquoise scarf was draped across the mannequin in the window. Jessica sighed, lamenting her fate. *Maybe if I bought that scarf, I would cheer up,* she thought. After all, she still had some money left over from buying the party decorations. *No,* she told herself finally, *you don't deserve it!* And besides, it probably cost more than it looked. After all, this was Evita's, a boutique where only the Lila Fowlers of this world could afford to shop.

Miserably Jessica turned away from the window

and walked down the street, her shoulders slumped in defeat. It was no use: Elizabeth was leaving, and Jessica couldn't do a thing about it. It was time to face the facts.

Sighing, Jessica paused for a moment and plopped the heavy bags she was carrying onto a roadside bench. They were filled with party decorations from Occasions, the most sophisticated store in town. Jessica had bought deep red linen tablecloths, piles of long, slender candles in the same shade, and strings of twinkling red lights, as well as a mirror ball for the dance floor. She had also ordered long-stemmed red roses for the centerpiece of the buffet table and last—*and* most expensively—an exquisite ice sculpture shaped like a Greek goddess that at this very moment was being sculpted for the event.

But none of these things could cheer Jessica up. It was useless. Even the party that she was so looking forward to, the party that would reinforce her position at the very pinnacle of the social pyramid, couldn't lift her spirits.

Grudgingly Jessica picked up her bag, groaning at the weight of it, and moved off in the direction of campus. It was time to start decorating Theta house, and whether or not she felt like it, Jessica knew she had to get going.

As she passed Style 1, Jessica looked in through the doors, more out of habit than interest. Their clothes were generally too boring for Jessica's taste. Too much beige and shapeless floral dresses that made Jessica think of milkmaids and peasants and library-loving nerds—basically the wallflowers of this world. Definitely not stylish enough for Jessica. But just before she passed by, something caught her eye.

"Nick!" she whispered.

Stopping, Jessica squinted to get a better look. Yes, it was definitely the one and only Nick Fox talking to a cashier who was holding up chinos and polo shirts.

Oh no! Jessica thought in a panic. *Please, oh please, let me be hallucinating!* But sadly, she realized she wasn't seeing things. Nick was transforming into Joe College before her very eyes—and to add insult to injury, he was shopping at the most boring store in Sweet Valley!

Irritated, Jessica hurried away before Nick had a chance to spot her. She didn't feel like talking to him or anyone else for that matter. Moving quickly, Jessica rounded the corner and smacked right into someone tall, skinny, and easy to knock over.

"Jessica!" Winston cried. "Yeow! I think I broke something."

"Well, try watching where you're going next time, OK, Winnie?" she snapped.

"Whoa! Sorry, bulldozer woman," Winston replied amiably, holding a grocery bag to his chest. "Anyway, I'm glad I ran into you because I

159

can fill you in about how dinner's coming along. Everything's great, just super, just really—it really is—just great." Winston smiled broadly and put his hand on Jessica's arm. "You don't have *one thing* to worry about."

Yeah, right! Jessica thought angrily. *Only my sister leaving me and my boyfriend entering Geek City limits. Not one thing to worry about!*

"I've got to get going, Winston," she said abruptly, rubbing her aching elbow. *Why couldn't he watch his step?* she thought irritably. *Because he was too busy thinking about himself to look out for others.* Just like everyone else in Jessica's life.

Winston moved toward the parking lot behind the shopping center. He had to hurry. Denise would be going crazy wondering what he had found to replace the lobster.

Crossing the parking lot, Winston took out his car keys. "Hey, Winston!" someone called out, and he looked up to see Nick unlocking his Camaro. "How're you doing?" Nick asked.

"Uh, good," Winston replied, his nerves tensing. *I'd better watch my step,* he told himself. *One false move and Nick will see what's in this bag. Then he'll tell Jess, and then Denise and I will be done for!*

"What've you been up to? Buying stuff for the party?" Nick added, gesturing at Winston's bag.

"No," Winston replied a little too quickly. *Careful,* he warned himself. *This guy is a cop. A*

160

detective! If I act nervous or look suspicious, he'll pick up on it!

"Oh, I'm just restocking my groceries," Winston said breezily. "You know, Denise cleared out my *entire fridge*," he added with a smile. "Vegetable, animal, or mineral, it's all gone!" He prayed he was coming off as casual because inside, his heart was pounding. He was pretty sure it was against the law to lie to a cop!

"Well, I'll see you later," Nick said, getting into his car. "I'm looking forward to the party."

That makes one of us, Winston thought as he waved good-bye. *I'm looking forward to it being over!*

"Hair up or down?" Jessica asked Elizabeth. "What do you think? I've *got* to look stunning tonight. After all, I'm the hostess with the mostess."

Elizabeth smiled affectionately at her sister, who was standing in her underwear in front of the full-length mirror, clutching a fistful of hairpins in one hand and a can of hair spray the size of a fire extinguisher in the other.

"You look beautiful no matter what," Elizabeth insisted.

"Thanks, Liz, but that doesn't help!" Jessica retorted. "Although why I'm asking you, whose hair is in a perpetual ponytail, I don't know." Jessica shook her head with a rueful smile. "You know something? This . . . this feels weird."

"What does?" Elizabeth smoothed her stockings and looked back at Jessica, caught by the wistful tone in her voice.

"Us getting ready for a party together. Maybe for the last time." Jessica sat down on the bed beside Elizabeth.

"Oh, Jess. Don't be so melodramatic. I'm not leaving tonight!" Elizabeth forced herself to sound bright and teasing, but inside she felt a wave of nostalgia engulf her. *Don't show it,* she commanded herself. *You have to be strong for Jessica.*

"Well, I just wonder if we'll ever have a chance to do this again," Jessica replied in a small voice, twisting her hands in her lap.

"Of *course* we will!" Elizabeth took Jessica's hands in hers and squeezed them. "There will be plenty of other opportunities for our ritual getting-ready sessions. I'm only leaving at the end of the semester, and besides, it's not like I'm moving to Siberia, you know. I'll come back for vacations, and you'll visit me. There'll be lots of other parties."

"I hope you're right." Jessica gave Elizabeth a sad, longing look and then turned away with a sigh. "Anyway, I suppose I'd better cheer up and enjoy it while I can."

"Oh, Jess . . ." Elizabeth sighed too. She didn't know what else to say. She didn't know how to comfort her twin. Or herself.

"Well, at least I won't have to argue with you

over what you're wearing anymore," Jessica joked. "Although I must say," she added, "that burgundy velvet dress you're wearing is gorgeous." Jessica eyed Elizabeth with approval. "Didn't I pick that out for you, like, a million years ago?"

"Yes," Elizabeth replied, and turned to Jessica to be zipped up. *It sure does feel like forever . . . and then again, just like it was yesterday.*

The dress was the same one Elizabeth had almost thrown out days earlier—the velvet dress she'd worn to a dance with Tom. Elizabeth looked in the mirror, almost regretting her decision to keep it. *But I did it for a reason,* she reminded herself. *I did it because I have to acknowledge the past and accept it, good and bad.*

Besides, it was a lovely dress. *And it's appropriate,* Elizabeth thought wryly, *and ironic that I should be wearing it to my own good-bye party.* She smoothed the dress over her hips, a pinch of pain clutching at her heart as she felt the soft fabric. *My good-bye dress,* she thought sadly. *A symbol of what I once had and what I'm now leaving behind.*

With a heavy heart Elizabeth found her thoughts floating to Tom. For a moment this afternoon she'd thought she was getting through to him. Just for a second it seemed as if the cold freeze between them was finally beginning to thaw. And then Dana had come along and ruined it all. The minute she put her arm through his, Tom's face changed. It was like the real Tom was exposed one moment, and the next a heavy door had slammed shut. After that, Tom remained impassive, not even acknowledging Elizabeth when she walked away.

Was I just imagining it? Elizabeth asked herself. *Or was there the flicker of surrender in his eyes? Was he trying to reach out to me too?* It was impossible to tell. And it probably didn't matter anyway. Elizabeth was leaving, and their fate was sealed.

"Liz. You look kind of faraway," Jessica said, interrupting Elizabeth's silent dialogue. "Here, let me help you with your makeup. Go and sit at the dresser. You know I'm killer when it comes to painting faces!"

Elizabeth laughed, grateful for Jessica's enthusiasm as she bustled around, grabbing lipstick and mascara wands and emptying bags full of eye shadow onto the dresser. As usual Jessica was making a huge mess, and for once Elizabeth was glad of it, even finding it comforting.

Jessica would never change. She would always be a handful; she would always be impulsive. And she would always be there for Elizabeth. At least that was one thing Elizabeth knew she could count on. And with all the changes that were taking place, it was nice to know that some things would always stay the same.

But as Jessica began applying foundation and powder to Elizabeth's face, Elizabeth felt something tugging at her deep inside. How many more moments *would* there be like this? When *would* she and Jessica have their next precious ritual face painting, hair fixing, and outfit arranging?

"There you go." Jessica breathed quietly as she applied the last streak of eyeliner to Elizabeth's closed eyelids. "You can open now."

Elizabeth opened her eyes and found herself looking into the mirror, her face beside Jessica's. Jessica had done a wonderful job. Elizabeth looked sophisticated and glamorous—her skin flawless, her lips glossy with ruby-colored lipstick—but she didn't look overdone.

"Thanks, Jess. I feel great." Elizabeth regarded herself solemnly. *That's a lie,* she thought. *I don't feel great. I feel like my heart is breaking.*

Without her even saying a word, Elizabeth could tell that Jessica knew what she was feeling as they looked at themselves soberly in the mirror. Their identical faces stared back at them, and for almost a full minute neither spoke. They were both too caught up in the bittersweetness of the moment, a moment that, like these final days, was passing far too swiftly.

"Tofu!" Denise screeched as she opened the bag Winston had brought in. "Tofu. Tofu-tofu-tofu," she repeated in disbelief. "That's, like, one step away from seaweed . . . and a *trillion* steps away from *lobster!*"

"Shhh! Don't blow our cover!" Winston cried. "Just calm down."

"Calm down?" Denise yelled, her voice rising even more than before. "You bring me tofu and I'm supposed to be *calm?"*

"Well, like I even had a choice!" Winston replied. "I mean, *you* try coming up with a delicious but cheap alternative to lobster. You're asking for a miracle here, Denise, and in case you haven't noticed, I'm just one guy with a sad excuse for a bank account."

Denise bit her lip. "I'm sorry, Winnie. You're right. I was asking too much." Sighing heavily, she picked up the tofu and carried it to the chopping board. "We have no choice, I guess. It's tofu or nothing."

"Denise, you're a brilliant cook, and you know it. Once you mix everything up and spice it, no one will even notice the difference?" Winston offered, trying to be helpful.

"Please! Tofu versus lobster? What fool wouldn't know the difference?" Flustered, Denise turned away from Winston and began chopping. She wasn't meaning to take out her frustration on him, but sometimes he *did* seem a little clueless. After all, who couldn't tell succulent lobster from rubbery, tasteless tofu?

"I wouldn't know the difference," Winston added. "But I guess I'm no connoisseur." He picked up a limp stalk of asparagus and held it up. "I mean, give me a nice juicy burger over this stuff any day!"

Despite her mood, Denise couldn't help smiling. Winston always managed to cheer her up somehow. Still, she was extremely anxious. A lot was riding on her cooking being top-notch, and with a mistake like this lobster thing, Denise was pretty certain that her dreams of impressing people with her food and then getting catering jobs were about to go up in smoke.

It's no use, she thought miserably as she slammed the knife into a block of tofu. *Jessica will be furious, and everyone will hate my food! And on top of everything, I haven't just wasted the Wakefields' money but my own and Winston's too. Money we don't even have!*

"I still think when the tofu's spiced up, cooked, and tossed in with the salad stuff, no one will notice," said Winston.

Denise looked up at him doubtfully and resumed her chopping, banging the knife down extra hard. *Not only will they notice—they'll never let me live it down. I'll be the laughingstock of Theta house!* With an explosion of anger Denise hurled the knife into a large block of the nasty white stuff. Silently cursing it, she continued to chop with a vengeance.

It was going to be a long night.

Chapter
Ten

"Liz, hi! You look great!"

Elizabeth's face flushed with pleasure as she heard her brother Steven's voice. She looked up to see him and his girlfriend, Billie Winkler, come through the Theta house doorway. "Steven, I'm so glad you're here," she said as her brother enveloped her in a crushing hug.

"Are you doing OK?" Steven asked, giving Elizabeth a searching look. Steven always seemed to know when Elizabeth wasn't her usual self. He was a very protective older brother, and Elizabeth had always gone to him with her problems. But not this time. She knew that only she would be able to sort out her feelings about leaving. No one else could help her.

"I'm fine, Steven," Elizabeth replied, flashing a broad smile. Truthfully, despite the festive atmosphere of the party, she wasn't any happier than she'd been earlier while getting ready with Jessica. And no matter how much she tried to lighten up, Elizabeth couldn't stop her mental gymnastics.

"This is quite a turnout, Liz," Billie said, looking coolly elegant, her neat dark bob swinging softly at her neck. She hugged Elizabeth warmly, taking her away from her thoughts, if only for a moment.

It was true. As Elizabeth scanned the room she felt a warm glow spread through her. Almost everyone she had ever met at SVU was there, and still more people were arriving in swarms every minute. And Jessica had truly outdone herself with the decorating. The room was bathed in a soft rosy glow from the candles and twinkling lights, and mellow music floated through the air. Elizabeth smiled as she caught sight of Jessica, laughing and twirling her punch glass, her hair piled into an elegant chignon. The perfect host.

"Congratulations, Elizabeth!"

Elizabeth turned to see Lila standing behind her, looking drop-dead gorgeous in a dramatic and very expensive-looking black dress with a plunging neckline, diamonds the size of grapes glinting in her ears. Bruce was at her elbow, his steel blue eyes even more piercing than usual against the black of his perfectly tailored dinner jacket.

"We brought you a few little things." Bruce thrust two packages wrapped in silver-and-black paper into Elizabeth's hands. "Open them."

Elizabeth felt a warm flush singe her cheeks. Lila *and* Bruce *buying* me *presents! That's a first!* Although she could tolerate their company, Elizabeth often found Bruce and Lila too snobby and superficial to be close friends. But looking at them now, she felt a surge of affection for them. They'd been in her life, in some annoying form or another, for as long as she could remember.

"You shouldn't have!" Elizabeth crowed in delight as she fingered a soft, leather-bound day planner.

"You're going to need to look professional," Bruce added as Elizabeth kissed him on the cheek. "Now open the next one."

As Elizabeth unveiled a small, slim box Bruce grabbed it from her and pulled it open, revealing a digital address book. "This is for you to carry on your assignments. You see," he continued, pressing buttons, "you can log in all your sources' phone numbers, and it fits right into your pocket."

"Of course, I wanted to get you something more glamorous," Lila interjected, "but Bruce insisted on these dull, practical gifts, and then I realized he was right. These are *perfect* for you."

"Oh, Lila." Elizabeth laughed, hugging her tightly. "You always know exactly what to say!" *I never thought I'd see the day when I'd miss Lila's tactless comments,* Elizabeth thought ruefully, *but I guess that day is about to arrive!*

"There's some delivery guy at the door for you," Denise called out as she passed by, her arms laden with trays of hot snacks for the buffet table. Elizabeth went to the door and found a messenger clutching a large gorilla-gram.

"Who's it from?" Nina asked as she and Alex looked over Elizabeth's shoulder.

"'Congratulations to our reporting star. We'll miss you, but we'll be watching as you shoot to the top. All our love, Mom and Dad,'" Elizabeth read as Alex squeezed the stuffed gorilla that had held the message.

"It's so cute!" Alex squealed.

Elizabeth looked at the gorilla-gram and felt a lump forming in her throat. Everyone had made an effort to make her feel special. But all it did was remind her of what she would be leaving behind.

"Hi, beautiful!" Scott squeezed Elizabeth's shoulders and winked at her. He looked good in a dark green suede jacket, his thick blond hair shining. *You're not leaving* everyone *behind*, Elizabeth reminded herself as Scott's lips touched hers for a quick kiss. Somehow the thought didn't make her feel better, though she made sure it didn't show. She didn't want to upset Scott, and she *certainly* didn't want Jessica—who was hovering nearby—to see how sad she was, especially after all the trouble she'd taken to arrange such a great party.

"May I have this dance?" Scott asked, taking Elizabeth's hand.

"Sure, why not?" Elizabeth pasted a brave smile on her face and allowed Scott to lead her onto the dance floor, which was crowded with couples. Just before she took Scott's hand, she felt a gentle tap at her shoulder.

"Liz!" She turned to see a familiar face: Todd, looking handsome in a navy linen blazer that emphasized the lines of his sculpted shoulders. "You look gorgeous."

"Not so bad yourself!" Elizabeth replied, giving Todd a grateful smile. A bittersweet pang shot through her chest as she looked into Todd's eyes. Todd. Uncomplicated and sincere. Her very first love and oldest friend. She would miss him.

"Save a dance for me?" Todd asked tenderly, and Elizabeth knew he was feeling a similar sadness.

"Always," she murmured. *We'll always have a strong connection,* she thought, and she could tell by Todd's expression that he was thinking much the same. As she watched Todd walk away Elizabeth felt the knot in her chest loosen. He supported her decision, and she knew that down the road, he would still be there for her, no matter where she was and what she was doing, and she would be there for him.

Scott pulled Elizabeth close. As they began to move to the music Elizabeth felt her heart flutter and the tension in her body ease. The pressure of Scott's strong arms around her waist and the way his clear blue eyes roved lazily over her body produced a

173

dizzying effect. But after only a minute, from deep inside, a small but doubting voice stopped Elizabeth from fully enjoying being in Scott's arms.

Do you really want to be here? it asked. *Does this really feel right?*

This small but insidious voice made Elizabeth feel more confused than ever. On the one hand, Scott was everything she needed—smart, sexy, and attentive—and yet Elizabeth still couldn't totally relax with him. Some part of her was always outside of the experience, questioning and doubting.

Why do you make things so complicated for yourself? Elizabeth wondered, irritated that her analytical brain couldn't stop ticking for even a moment to let her enjoy her party. But it was useless. Elizabeth knew that right up until the moment she left Sweet Valley and probably even after that, she would be plagued by "what if" questions about everything: Scott, leaving, Tom. . . .

Almost as if on cue, Tom bobbed into sight on the dance floor, and Elizabeth felt the breath catch in her throat. She had seen him arrive, but he'd avoided her so far, and Elizabeth hadn't wanted to approach him. Especially not with Dana stuck to him as if she were wearing Krazy Glue.

Elizabeth felt a bolt of jealousy and annoyance flash through her as she watched them together. Dana, barely clothed in a tiny lime minidress, was practically wrapped around him, her hands

174

clamped to his back. And Tom didn't look too un-happy with the situation. Furious, Elizabeth glared at Tom, drilling her eyes into him as she watched him nuzzle Dana's neck. After a moment he looked up, caught Elizabeth's gaze, and held it with his own.

It wasn't a look of smug self-satisfaction or anger or hatred but a look of . . . something else. *What is it?* Elizabeth wondered in frustration. Regret? Fear? Sadness? *What is he feeling?* At last Tom broke the stare and moved away, and Elizabeth contemplated the blank spot on the dance floor in a daze. Did Tom understand what she had been trying to tell him that afternoon? And would he ever admit it if he did?

As with everything else right now, Elizabeth couldn't find an answer.

"Hors d'oeuvre?" Winston inquired in a mock French accent as he pointed to the buffet table piled high with snacks.

"Wow. It all looks great," Nick said, scanning the colorful array: breads and dips of various kinds, potato skins stuffed with vegetables and cheese, grilled asparagus, and an intriguing-looking salad.

"I'll try the salad," Nick decided. "It looks really good."

"I'm more of an asparagus man myself," Winston broke in quickly. "Why don't you have some? I grilled it, and I must say, it is truly excellent."

"In that case I'll pass." Nick chuckled as he piled some salad onto a small plate. "I think I'd rather eat something Denise made, if that's OK by you. No offense or anything!" He put a forkful of lettuce and what looked like some kind of marinated crab into his mouth and chewed. It was OK, mild and a bit tasteless . . . definitely not crab. "What is this?"

"Uh, it's lobster *al* Denise," Winston replied, ramming a piece of seafood into his mouth. "Mmmm, isn't it delicious? She sure is a gourmet."

"Yeah," Nick replied, "it's pretty good." Actually he wasn't too impressed. For all the fuss people made of it, Nick couldn't see what the big deal was about lobster. It was pretty disappointing for all the hype. As far as he was concerned, it was rubbery and didn't have much taste for something that cost so much. Nick was convinced everyone just made a big fuss over it because it was expensive. As for Nick, he would take canned tuna over lobster any day of the week.

As he swallowed the last of his salad and reached out for something to take away the taste, Nick's eye caught Jessica's and he smiled appreciatively as she came over to him, looking phenomenal in a sexy navy dress and some kind of smoky eye makeup. Nick felt a burst of pride. *That's* my *girlfriend,* he thought with pleasure, picking up on the longing looks Jessica received as she walked

176

past groups of guys. Jessica was certainly not the easiest person to handle, but Nick was completely smitten. She was exciting and hotheaded, just the kind of girl he wanted. Not some doormat or shrinking violet who waited on him hand and foot. "Hi, sweetheart," he said when Jessica arrived at his side. "You look incredible."

"Hi," Jessica replied, looking Nick over. "And you look very . . . academic."

"Do you like it? I'm practicing," Nick added with a laugh, holding out his arms. He was wearing chinos and a button-down shirt, like half of the guys at the party. A definite change from his usual style. "Now that I'm taking a break from the force, I can start dressing better," he continued. "Just think, you won't have to see me looking all bleary-eyed and unshaven in jeans and a T-shirt after a heavy day on the beat."

"Well, actually, that's the Nick I know and love." Jessica grabbed a carrot stick and began to nibble on it delicately. "But suit yourself." She looked irresistible standing there, and Nick felt a wave of love wash over him.

Nick moved over to Jessica and wrapped his arms around her waist. "Mmmm, you look good enough to eat," he murmured, his lips grazing her ear. "What's the matter?" he added as Jessica wriggled out of his grasp and grabbed another carrot stick. This wasn't like her. If anyone loved affection and attention, it was Jessica.

"Sorry," Jessica replied brusquely. "But I can't concentrate on you right now. It's this *party*. It's making me realize that Elizabeth is really leaving. Now it finally feels real."

"Don't worry," Nick replied, stroking her hair. "You'll be OK. I'll make sure of that."

"I'd better get back to the door," Jessica said as she gently removed his hand from her hair. "Isabella just arrived, and I need to talk to her. I'll see you later." She gave a little wave before she moved off.

Well, at least it's not me, Nick thought as he swiped a stalk of celery through a creamy dip. Still, Jessica's mood bothered him a little, and Nick couldn't help looking forward to Elizabeth's departure. *Then it will be over,* he thought. *Jessica will have to accept it, and we can get on with our lives . . . together.*

"I love dancing with you," Dana murmured into Tom's neck. "We move so well together."

Not as well as Elizabeth and I used to, Tom thought. He stole a glance at Elizabeth, but he couldn't see her properly and all he got was a flash of her dark red dress. Tom loved that dress. It reminded him of the time he'd last seen Elizabeth in it, at a dance. They had been so in tune that night and had danced and danced for hours. It seemed like a hundred years ago.

What is she thinking? Tom wondered. Their

eyes had met a few minutes back, but her expression was unreadable. She looked cozy enough with Scott, but Tom wasn't sure. And he didn't want to be convinced.

There's only one way to find out, he mused. If there was a gap, if there was a chance, now was the time to seize it. Tom took a deep breath and gently disengaged himself from Dana's embrace. "I'd better go and say hi to Elizabeth," he muttered, not meeting Dana's eyes. He couldn't deal with guilt right now. "I'll be back in a moment."

His heart knocking nervously at his rib cage, Tom forced himself to cross the dance floor to where Scott and Elizabeth were standing. "May I cut in for a moment?" he asked, addressing Scott stiffly.

Scott's face darkened and Elizabeth broke their embrace, looking surprised. For a moment no one said anything. Then Scott looked searchingly at Elizabeth.

"Um, just for a minute, Scott," Elizabeth finally said, licking her lips nervously.

"Fine," Scott replied smoothly, and stepped back. "I'll go get a drink."

Tom could tell Scott was trying to control his anger, but his brittle voice gave him away. And Tom felt good. It was his first, admittedly small victory of the evening, but a victory nonetheless.

Nervously Tom took Elizabeth's hand. It was cold, and she regarded him impassively before looking at the floor. Soft, romantic music filled the air, but Tom could only register the tension between them. Neither one spoke, and they moved awkwardly, so differently from the last time they'd danced together.

Tom felt his fingers tremble as they touched the soft velvet of Elizabeth's dress. He moved a hand to the warm, smooth skin of Elizabeth's back, the feeling of her skin causing a sharp pain of longing in his heart, as if he'd been pierced with a glass splinter. At the same time he felt her stiffen in his arms, her body growing taut. *Is she recoiling from me? Or is it just the shock of touching after such a long time?* Finally, unable to bear the silence a moment longer, Tom cleared his throat. "Congratulations," he said in a low voice.

Elizabeth's eyelids fluttered and she looked up at Tom, surprise on her face. "Thank you," she responded quietly, her face quickly resuming its impenetrable expression. "That means a lot coming from you," she added.

For a moment Tom felt his blood quicken. *Is she being sarcastic?* he wondered. *Because if she is, then I give up.*

But as he looked into her eyes, Tom could see a glimmer of feeling. Elizabeth was being genuine. It *did* mean a lot. Emboldened, Tom pulled Elizabeth closer, feeling a tingling in his chest as he inhaled her sweet, familiar perfume. She didn't pull away like he'd thought she would but instead tightened her arms around his neck.

Tom closed his eyes, and again he gently moved his hand up above Elizabeth's waist to the soft, milky skin of her back. Still Elizabeth didn't pull back. Tom felt confused but hopeful. What was she trying to tell him? One moment she breathed hot, the next cold. What was he meant to make of it all? Searching her face for further proof, Tom found himself even more conflicted. Elizabeth wouldn't look up at him again. *What are you feeling now?* Tom begged silently. *Tell me*.

At that moment the music changed from a soft, intimate slow number to a raucous classic. All of a sudden it seemed as if the whole party crowded onto the dance floor, and Tom and Elizabeth were sandwiched between dozens of jumping, whooping bodies.

"Elizabeth!" Tom shouted, but the music was too loud, and before long Elizabeth was swept away by a crowd of friends to dance in a group. Defeated, Tom pushed his way angrily past the thick crowd and finally broke through to an empty space off the dance floor, cursing silently. He had been so close to finding out how Elizabeth felt, and then the music had changed.

Desperately Tom searched the dance floor for Elizabeth, but it was no use. He couldn't find her. At that moment Tom felt like the loneliest person on earth. He'd had his chance, but it hadn't worked out. He stared at the crowd, willing

Elizabeth to appear, searching one last time for a flash of her dress, a glimmer of her shining blond hair. *If there's any hope at all,* he prayed, *let me find her. Let me just see her.* Tom closed his eyes and then opened them, willing Elizabeth to come into his line of vision.

Nothing. She was lost in a sea of faces. *Gone,* Tom thought sadly, and turned away, jamming his hands into his pockets. *She's gone forever.*

Chapter Eleven

"Does this look any better?" Denise asked Winston, stepping back from painting a mixture of butter and paprika onto some tofu to make it look red, like cooked lobster meat.

"Definitely," Winston replied. "And anyway, I just saw Nick eating it and he said it was good, so there you go."

"Yeah, well, it's not Nick I'm worried about. It's Jessica." Denise frowned and dabbed more butter to the side of a piece of tofu. "Just keep everyone out of the kitchen," she told Winston. "I don't want anyone nosing around."

Winston kissed the side of Denise's neck. "Roger!"

Denise stopped for a moment and took a deep breath, wiping her brow with her hand. All the cooking and worrying was exhausting her. *But it will all be worth it*, she thought, picturing the compliments and catering jobs that would be coming her way. *If I can just hold out a little longer and keep suspicion at bay, then everything will work out.*

"It's OK, Denise," Winston continued, pulling a tray from the oven. "We've got everything under control. Everyone's raving about how amazing the food is. And if my opinion helps, let me tell you, that cheese fondue is killer. It went down like a homesick mole!"

Denise laughed and looked at Winston tenderly. He really *had* helped her during her darkest hour.

"You're a hit, honey!" Winston said reassuringly. "Don't worry, everything is going great."

Maybe he's right! Denise thought, relaxing her shoulders. *We just might be able to pull this off.* And it was true, judging by the empty trays that Winston kept bringing to the kitchen. "Now if we can just keep everyone out of the—"

"Hellooo, Martha Stewart," a silvery voice trilled from the doorway. Denise froze. It sounded like Jessica. She didn't want to turn around. "Brother," she muttered to Winston under her breath, "now we're in for it."

"Hi, Lila! Hi, Bruce!" Winston bellowed jovially.

So it's not Jessica, Denise thought in relief. Still, Lila wasn't good news either. First of all, she and Jessica were joined at the hip, and if Lila smelled a rat, it would get back to Jessica faster than the speed of light. And second, Lila was pretty nosy, so chances were *she* would pick up on the lobster scam.

Denise felt her heart began to beat faster. She hunched her body over the tofu and kept her head down. "Get them out of here," she hissed to Winston as Bruce strolled over to the kitchen counter, drink in hand.

"I'll do my best," Winston whispered before turning to Bruce and Lila. He clapped a hand on Bruce's shoulder and pointed him in the direction of a steaming tray of asparagus and quiche waiting on the sideboard. "Quick, grab one," Winston said, pointing at the quiche. "They're piping hot. And if you wouldn't mind, I could do with a hand, Patman. Would you take that tray out to the buffet table for me?"

"Sure thing," Bruce replied. "After I offer my compliments to the chef. Well done, Denise. This is a real feast. Almost as good as my aunt Chantal's summer cooking in the Hamptons, back East."

"And that's high praise coming from Bruce," Lila chimed in. "Like me, he has eaten some of the best, most exotic foods the world has to offer. I congratulate you, Denise."

And I thank you, but you could you please get lost? Denise thought as she flashed Lila a nervous smile and casually threw some spinach on top of the tofu in front of her. Trust Lila to come in and meddle! But despite herself Denise couldn't help being amused by Lila and Bruce's big talk.

"Now, Denise, I've had your vegetables julienne," Lila began, exaggerating her French accent, "and I've tried all the other delectable hors d'oeuvres." She sauntered over to where Denise stood, a piece of asparagus dangling between her long, manicured fingers. "But what I'm *really* looking forward to is the lobster. Jessica told me you were busy preparing some more, and I simply *must* try it before I miss out again. I adore lobster!"

"It's my favorite food," Bruce added. "I can't go for more than a few weeks without some fresh lobster tail."

"We certainly know our seafood, Bruce and I," Lila said, smiling at Bruce. "So I think you should let us do the taste test!"

Cripes! Denise gave Winston a pleading look, and he shrugged helplessly. If Lila and Bruce were really the connoisseurs of seafood they claimed to be—and as the two richest students at SVU the chances were high—then Denise and Winston were in big trouble. If Lila and Bruce got near the tofu, their cover would be blown and the rest would be history!

"So where is it?" Lila demanded, wrinkling her pretty nose and sniffing the air. "I think I can smell it, but I don't see it."

That's because it isn't there! Denise thought,

186

turning her back to the countertop to protect the tofu from sight.

"There it is!" Bruce announced as he walked over to a pan sizzling on the stove. In horror Denise watched as Bruce's hand neared the pan. How could she have been so dumb? She was so busy trying to hide the tofu on the countertop, she'd forgotten the pile cooking on the stove in plain sight.

Bruce snapped up a sliver of fake lobster in a second, but to Denise it seemed like an eternity. "Here goes!"

Here goes my reputation, *that is . . . and my plans to get out of debt . . . and my plans to stay in school,* she thought grimly as Bruce opened his mouth and dangled the stick of white, rubbery, tasteless "seafood" above it. *Good-bye, money. Good-bye, loans. Good-bye, SVU.*

Nick chewed on an olive as he listened to Steven's words with interest. Steven was a great person to talk to about studying law since he had already taken a lot of classes and knew what Nick would someday be headed for.

"Law really is a kick," Steven enthused as he refilled his punch glass. "I just know it's the right profession for me. I need something that keeps me on my toes, you know?"

"Exactly," Nick replied energetically. Working for the police had gotten Nick addicted to a fast-paced, unpredictable, active lifestyle. It was the bloodcurdling danger that had been turning him off in recent weeks. All those close scrapes with Jessica at his side were too terrifying for him to want to relive. But he didn't want to give up working for law, order, and justice. Nick had figured that becoming a lawyer would afford him the same kinds of thrills without the life-threatening risks; judging from the way Steven was talking about the profession, Nick was right. "So tell me about the assignments," he urged.

"Well, there's a ton of them. I've pulled some serious all-nighters this year."

"Tell me about it," Nick replied with a laugh. "All the car chases, stakeouts, drug busts . . . it's a real rush."

"Well, this isn't exactly the same game, Nick," Steven replied.

"Good." Nick picked another olive from the salad on his plate. "I'm burned out right now, so I'm taking a leave of absence. I figure I need something a little less strenuous to pursue in my life. Unless I want to die young of a heart attack or . . . something worse."

"Well, you can forget car chases. Right now it's just paper chases. Paper after paper . . . I'm doing tax law at the moment, and it's heavy on the brain, but not the body."

"Tax law," Nick repeated skeptically. "It sounds kind of boring."

"Well, it *is* heavy. But not as heavy as the business

law course I just finished. It took me forever to work out the differences between all the state and federal laws. I spent weekends wading through copyright disputes, takeovers, and bankruptcies. By the end of it I couldn't even do the dishes without seeing figures floating in the dishwater. It completely takes over your life, Nick. You have to be one hundred percent dedicated."

"Huh. Really." Copyright. Bankruptcy. Nick didn't enjoy the sound of that. *I'd have more fun stamping packages for FedEx,* he thought. "Tell me about your lectures," he suggested. Maybe those would be more interesting.

"Well," said Steven, "right now I'm really lucky. I got into an amazing class on civil law with a great professor."

"Do you get to discuss trials and pose fake courts in the classroom?" Nick asked. *This* sounded more like it.

Steven laughed and lightly punched Nick on the shoulder. "Sorry, buddy, but you've been watching too much *Matlock.* Most of our discussions involve petty civil suits and the intricacies of litigation. No crimes of passion. Not yet anyway."

"Oh." Nick was disappointed. The more Steven talked, the more boring it sounded. *Maybe I'm making a mistake,* he thought. The thought hadn't occurred to him before. When he decided to leave the force to take classes, Nick felt sure he was doing the right thing. There wasn't much doubt in his mind. Not until now, that was.

". . . and it's long, long hours in the library," Steven continued. "But it's still pretty exciting stuff, I think."

"Sounds . . . thought provoking," Nick replied. *Meaning dull.* But he didn't want to insult Jessica's brother. Smiling politely, Nick asked Steven more questions, all the while feeling his stomach sinking as he heard the disappointing answers. *Maybe everything will seem boring after the force,* Nick considered. There weren't many professions that could match up when it came to adrenaline rushes, that was for sure. But wasn't that what Nick wanted to get away from?

Nick sighed. It was all too confusing. What did he want? Kicks or classes? A life full of criminals and nutcases or a corporate boardroom?

Then Nick thought of Jessica, and a smile lit up his face. *What am I worried about?* he thought in amusement. Life would never be dull with a girlfriend like Jessica Wakefield around to stir things up. Not even a class in corporate tax law—or whatever it was Steven was going on about—could cramp Nick's lifestyle. Nick grinned, thinking back to all the fights, hysterics, dramas, and passion they had already shared. Every day with Jessica was a blast.

Perhaps going prelaw would be a good move after all, he mused. *Then I can sit back, be a boring student, and let Jessica provide me with the spice of life!*

*　　*　　*

"Thank you, but I'll take that!" Winston told Bruce, grabbing the dangling piece of tofu and tossing it into his own mouth. "Mmmm. Denise, this lobster really is delish!" Winston said with a wink in her direction.

"Hey, Egbert, watch it," Bruce boomed good-naturedly. "That piece of lobster had my name on it."

"Did it?" Winston asked, his eyes wide and innocent behind his wire-rimmed glasses. "Whoops! Sorry, I didn't notice—and I *just couldn't resist*. Anyway, only the *chefs* are allowed to taste in the kitchen. *You* have to wait until it's out on the table, like all the other guests. Now go on," Winston finished, shepherding Bruce and Lila toward the door.

Denise breathed a sigh of relief. Thank goodness for Winston! He'd come in and saved the day just when Denise thought they were really done for. She glanced after Bruce and Lila. They were allowing Winston to lead them out. Good! Now Denise could get back to her tofu chopping in peace and quiet.

Suddenly, just as Denise was about to turn her back to the others, she saw Bruce dart back away from Winston toward the stove. "I'm not leaving without a taste!" he yelled, grinning and snatching up a piece of tofu. At that, Winston charged over to Bruce and tried to seize the "lobster," laughing all the way as if it were a big, funny joke. But

Denise could see that Winston was just as alarmed as she was.

"Sorry, Winston!" Bruce held the "lobster" high up in the air, and Winston jumped up and down, frantically trying to swat it. It was no use; Bruce was a full head taller than Winston. "Going, going . . . gone!" Bruce dropped the tofu into his mouth and chewed.

With bated breath Denise watched Bruce's face for some sign of an expression. *Maybe he won't notice,* she thought hopefully. But she knew that was wishful thinking. *Of course he'll notice, you fool!* Denise berated herself miserably. *If anyone would notice, it would be Bruce! He probably can tell the difference between California and Maine lobster in a taste test!* Cursing her luck, Denise could do nothing but stand and watch.

Bruce chewed slowly and looked at Denise, his face blank. Her heart skipped a beat and she steeled herself, waiting for the unavoidable.

Bruce swallowed. "Denise," he said, his voice low and even. "This is really, really good."

"Huh?" Denise was so shocked, she barely registered Bruce's words.

"It's excellent," Bruce continued. "The best lobster I've tasted since last summer in Maine."

"That's hard to beat," Lila chirped. "Maine has the best lobster in the *world*." She put her arm around Denise and gave her a squeeze. "Well done, hon."

"Try some, Li," Bruce offered, and before Denise could protest, he'd fed Lila a piece of tofu and she was chewing and looking thoughtful.

Uh-oh, Denise thought in dread. *Will Lila spot the truth, or will she follow Bruce's lead?*

Lila swallowed and turned to Bruce. "You're right. It's very good. The seasoning is different from the usual too. Bold and zesty . . . yet mild. Mmmm!"

Denise caught Winston's eye and almost erupted into giggles as Bruce chewed another piece of "lobster," nodding slowly.

"Mmmm," he said. "This really does rate as some of the finest lobster I've ever tried. And right now it can only be complemented by a glass of fine champagne. Come on, Lila, let's see if we can find some."

"I don't think we'll get lucky there," Lila replied with a toss of her lustrous brown hair. "This is a good party, but it's still only a college do. The drinks simply *aren't* in the Dom Pérignon league."

After Bruce and Lila left the kitchen, Denise fell into Winston's arms partly out of relief and partly in amusement. "I can't believe they fell for it," she said with a giggle.

"'The best I've had since Maine,'" Winston spoofed, putting on his best, snobbiest Bruce voice. "I almost cracked up right there."

"Lucky you didn't!" Denise smiled and giggled

193

uncontrollably. *Now my troubles are over,* she thought. *If I can fool one, I can fool them all!*

Jessica plucked a strawberry off a tray and looked around, pleased with herself. Everything was going beautifully. The party was sure to be the hit of the year, and Jessica would be known, once and for all, as *the* standard-bearer when it came to social occasions.

As she looked around the room she drank in the fruits of her labors. Well, sure, the other Thetas *had* helped, but *she* had spearheaded the entire function. It was easy to do one job, like Denise's, but hard to organize and coordinate everything.

And yet I did it, Jessica thought with a smile as her eyes swept over the decorations she'd picked out. The twinkling red lights, the smoky effects of all the soft candles, and the cherry on the top— the ice sculpture. It was without a doubt the most sophisticated and glamorous college party Sweet Valley had ever seen.

Jessica smiled happily. After this bash the Thetas would be known as the crème de la crème of campus society—as if there had been any doubt before. And who would be at the top of that select heap? Who was the one who put the sorority on the social map? Who was the Theta style compass? *Moi,* Jessica thought with satisfaction. *Yours truly. Me, me, me, me, me!*

Flicking her eyes across the hordes of people laughing, talking, dancing, and eating, Jessica's gaze fell on Elizabeth. She was dancing with Scott, and they looked very close.

A shadow was suddenly cast over Jessica's good mood. She didn't like Scott for a number of reasons. First, he was the one responsible for Elizabeth's hearing about the Colorado journalism program. Second, he was the one who encouraged Elizabeth to go. And third, Jessica just plain old didn't like him. There was something slippery in his manner, something untrustworthy. She couldn't put her finger on it exactly, but something was off.

Jessica trusted her instincts. When it came to men, she always prided herself on knowing what was what and who was who. And she was always right on target—except, perhaps, on the odd freak occasion.

Elizabeth, on the other hand, was far less experienced. *Not very worldly wise or sophisticated,* Jessica thought as she looked warily at her sister, *which is why I have to keep my eye on her.* Elizabeth had spent most of her time with the solid, boring type; Todd Wilkins was without a doubt the ancestral boyfriend, the mold from which all future SBTs would spring. *So how is she to know a rat when she sees one?* Jessica wondered, glaring at Scott. Now Tom Watts—he was only slightly less solid and boring than Todd, but he had for the most part been good for Elizabeth. Except for that nasty stuff that had happened after the breakup, Jessica hadn't minded him. And lately she had grown more and more convinced that Tom was the man for Elizabeth—mainly because he wasn't planning on taking Elizabeth anywhere far away. But as she watched her sister snuggling into Scott's chest, Jessica's wishful thinking seemed headed for crushing disappointment.

Jessica bit her lip. She'd hoped that by tonight Elizabeth and Tom would have made up, maybe even kissed or something. It was obvious that Elizabeth still cared for Tom, and Jessica had heard through the grapevine that Tom definitely hadn't gotten over Elizabeth either. But Tom was nowhere in sight.

What a shame, Jessica thought. *If they could just put the past behind them, then Elizabeth wouldn't want to leave.* Pouting, Jessica crossed her arms as she watched Scott pull Elizabeth to him. Where *was* Tom anyway? If he was still in love with Elizabeth, then why wasn't he trying to get her away from Scott? And why wasn't he trying to stop her from leaving SVU?

Am I the only one who cares? Jessica wondered irritably. *Do I have to do everything around here?*

"Hi, Jess!"

Jessica looked up to see Isabella saunter over. As usual she looked like a supermodel in a beautiful brown dress that fell softly to the floor and emphasized her slender figure. "The party's going well, isn't it?" Isabella said as she munched on a stuffed potato.

"I guess," Jessica replied, her eyes flitting back to the annoying sight of Scott and Elizabeth dancing together. "Although I'm getting tired of running around after everyone and everything," she added, her thoughts turning to Tom.

"What do you mean?" Isabella looked amused.

"I'm just getting sick of *doing* everything," Jessica repeated, ignoring Isabella as she raised an eyebrow.

It's true! I have to take care of a hundred things at once, Jessica thought. *And nobody takes care of me.*

She caught sight of Nick in the corner, talking to Steven, and frowned. Seeing Nick in his button-down oxford only reinforced her feelings. *Cops can take care of their girlfriends,* she thought, remembering how Nick had rescued her from prison. *But* students? *I don't* think *so!*

"I'll see you later," Jessica mumbled, leaving Isabella to go in search of Tom. Since he wasn't out there on the dance floor trying to win Elizabeth back, then he would simply have to be *brought* there.

Jessica scanned the crowd expertly, poked her head around corners, and even checked the line outside the bathroom. She was on a mission. Perhaps after a few inspirational words and some stretching of the truth, he could be coaxed into talking to Elizabeth.

I'll make up stuff, I'll stroke his ego, I'll spoon-feed him whatever lies he needs, Jessica thought. Anything was justified when it came to getting Elizabeth to stay. But Tom was nowhere to be found.

I hope he didn't leave, Jessica thought anxiously as she opened the door to the kitchen. "Hey, Denise, have you seen Tom?"

"He's not here," Denise replied, looking up from stirring vegetables. "Maybe he's outside," she offered, pointing her spatula in the direction of the back window.

Jessica moved over to the window and peered out. She saw a silhouette she couldn't recognize at first until it turned and a shaft of moonlight outlined the face.

Tom.

Tom is out there alone. He loves Elizabeth. I don't want Elizabeth to go, so . . .

She almost couldn't admit her scheme to herself, but already her mind was racing. Could it work?

Darting her eyes from side to side to check that no one was looking, Jessica slipped up the stairs and into the tiny spare bathroom. Luckily no one was up there. Locking the door behind her, she set to work, unpinning her hair and slicking her bangs back, trying not to catch her own eye in the mirror.

Part of her felt guilty for what she was about to do, but the other part—the part that was calling her to action—felt fine about it. It was necessary. *Anything* to prevent Elizabeth from leaving.

Even this.

I'm doing this for her, Jessica told herself. *And this is my one and only, my absolute last chance.* She swallowed hard to calm herself down as she slipped out of the bathroom and into the coat-room, glancing furtively around her.

Running her hands over the coat hooks, Jessica finally found the one she was looking for—a long, dark, plain coat. Elizabeth's coat. She pulled it on, making sure it hid her dress completely, and stole out into the back garden, her heart thumping.

The air was crisp and dewy, and Jessica shivered despite the coat. Tom was standing perfectly still, looking up at the sky, apparently deep in thought and unaware of Jessica's presence. As she drew near him Jessica took a deep breath. Would Tom pick up on her scam? Could she pull it off?

It's worked before, she told herself as she reached out a shaking hand to touch Tom's arm. *It will work again.*

Tom looked up at the moon, watching a single thread of silvery gray cloud move toward it as it glowed brightly in the dark sky. He sniffed in the cold air, inhaling the fresh, perfumed scent from the nearby flowering dogwood tree. It was a beautiful

199

night, he had to admit, even though he felt as if he couldn't properly appreciate it, even though he wished he were anywhere but in Sweet Valley right now. It was a night meant for romance, a night meant to be enjoyed by people in love. *Instead it's only me out here,* he thought sorrowfully. *Out here all alone.*

"Alone," he repeated softly to himself, hearing the word echo slightly in the empty yard and then die out.

Man, Watts, he thought with a groan. *Now you're really losing it! Talking to yourself. It's pathetic!* But no matter what he did, no matter how much fun he tried to have dancing with Dana or talking to his friends, he simply couldn't get rid of the loneliness and heartache he was feeling. He hadn't spoken to Elizabeth since they'd danced together—in fact he had avoided her all evening, but none of it helped. No matter what he did or how hard he tried to let it go, he couldn't. He was in love with Elizabeth, and it was tearing him apart.

Maybe if the music hadn't changed, I could have told her how I felt, Tom thought sadly. Not that it would have made any difference. Clearly Elizabeth had made her decision. She had moved on. Scott was in her life, and she was leaving Sweet Valley forever.

She only danced with you for old times' sake, Tom taunted himself bitterly. *Accept the facts. It wasn't*

200

anything more than a last dance. And Elizabeth's actions after the music changed only proved it. She hadn't tried to seek Tom out again; on the contrary, she'd spent the last hour in Scott's arms, and from what Tom had seen, she was perfectly happy about it too.

At that thought Tom felt his insides twist. The very notion of Elizabeth being happy with another guy—any guy, and especially a jerk like Scott—was enough to drive him crazy. And thinking about someone else holding her, stroking her silky hair and kissing her . . .

Stop it! Tom berated himself, trying to get his emotions in check, but he was powerless in the face of his feelings, which flooded over him, threatening to overwhelm him altogether.

Tom brought his hand up to his face and realized he was crying, hot tears falling to his cheeks. *You have to let go!* he ordered himself, angrily brushing his sleeve across his face. He had to stop remembering the past, analyzing the present, and dreaming of a future with Elizabeth. He had to stop dissecting every detail of their interactions. He had to stop caring. Thinking about Elizabeth—on any level—was pure torture, a pointless and very damaging obsession.

But despite trying to reason with himself, Tom knew that his feelings were beyond his control. Elizabeth had his heart in her hands, and he would simply have to ride it out and wait and hope for the day when his heartbreak would subside.

If such a day even existed.

A soft hand on his arm brought Tom out of his grief-stricken daze. He blinked guiltily. There was no need to hurt Dana further by showing how upset he was over Elizabeth. Dana had put up with enough of that already. Swallowing his tears, Tom forced a smile to his face and turned around. . . .

Elizabeth! Tom blinked, certain that he was seeing things. But there she was, right in front of him, her angelic face half lit, half shadowed by moonlight, her slight frame bundled into her favorite overcoat. Still, Tom couldn't believe it. The whole scenario—him out there in the garden all alone, yearning for Elizabeth, and then, without a word, her materializing at his side—was like a dream.

You're hallucinating, he told himself sternly, *you're creating a vision out of your desire. But you can't change reality!* He closed his eyes one more time and opened them. This time he was sure. Elizabeth *was* there, standing quietly, her soft hand trembling on Tom's arm. She *had* come for him after all.

"Elizabeth," Tom murmured in a whisper, as if speaking normally might shatter the moment. "It's really you."

She nodded and tightened her hold on Tom's

arm. Tom felt a lump rise in his throat as he looked at her. Had she come to comfort him? Had she come to say she was sorry that they couldn't be together? Or had she actually, finally come to tell him that she still loved him? He barely dared to consider the last possibility for fear that it wouldn't be true and once again he would be burned by Elizabeth. But looking at the tender, concerned expression in her eyes, he felt a rush of love for her, and he opened his mouth to say what was really in his heart. Tom had had enough of lying—to Elizabeth and himself.

"What would you do if I begged you not to leave?" Tom asked in a voice thick with emotion.

Elizabeth remained silent, and in that second as she looked at him, Tom felt like time had stretched for an hour. His heart pounded in his chest, and he felt as if he were about to faint.

Finally Elizabeth lowered her eyes from his, as if in preparation to say something. But without answering, she reached up and put her arms around Tom's neck. Then, pulling his face down toward her, she closed her eyes and brought her lips to his.

At the touch of Elizabeth's lips Tom felt as if he would drown in happiness, a warm tingling sensation overcoming his whole body. This word-less response was all he needed. Elizabeth's deep, soft kiss was as strong a seal of their love as any words could ever be.

Passionately Tom kissed her back with everything he had, giving to this moment every ounce of feeling he had reserved for Elizabeth, every tender and strong emotion he had had to hide for so long. *Finally,* Tom thought joyfully. Stroking Elizabeth's cheek, he pulled back for a moment to look into her eyes. There he saw all the reassurance he needed. This was no fantasy. She still loved him. The struggle between them was over.

Chapter Twelve

It's my *party,* Elizabeth thought. *So why do I feel so low?*

A line from a song floated into her head: *"It's my party, and I'll cry if I want to. . . ."* She smiled ruefully. *It's true. You're most alone when you're on center stage!*

Absentmindedly Elizabeth twirled the stem of her champagne glass in her fingers as she looked around the room. She was trying to concentrate on Scott's story about his last ski trip to Colorado, but her mind—and her eyes—were wandering. She was doing her best to enjoy the incredible party, but although she was smiling, laughing, and looking as if she were having a great time, Elizabeth couldn't shake the melancholy that gripped her inside.

"So then my dad hauled me up to this double black diamond and insisted I ski it," Scott continued. "And I gotta say, I even amazed myself. It's incredible what you can achieve when you really put your mind to it. Now I love skiing, and I can't wait to get back to the slopes of Vail. And next time," Scott added, smiling at Elizabeth, "it will be even better because I'm going to take you with me."

"Uh-huh," Elizabeth replied in a flat tone, searching the dance floor. Ever since she and Tom had been separated by the wave of enthusiastic people drawn by the loud, fast song, Elizabeth had been looking for him. But he seemed to have disappeared. It was such bad timing; Tom was obviously about to say something—something good and important, hopefully—and Elizabeth was finally going to understand what he felt for her. And then suddenly they were split up, and that was that. Still, being back in Tom's arms had felt so good while it lasted. Elizabeth recalled the way he'd held her—his arms firm yet gentle. *We just fit right together,* Elizabeth found herself thinking. *I miss that so much.*

But apparently Tom didn't, because he hadn't bothered to try to find her. Perhaps those strong feelings she'd thought he was about to divulge to her on the dance floor weren't so strong after all. Elizabeth felt her cheeks begin to burn—a hot, angry flush of frustration. Why did it all have to be so difficult? Why had Tom approached her and then vanished? Elizabeth shook her head in confusion. She couldn't understand any of it.

"Why are you shaking your head?" Scott asked, breaking Elizabeth's train of thought. "Don't you like skiing?"

"Uh, no," Elizabeth replied. "I mean, yes. I mean . . . I was just . . . thinking about something else. Sorry—I guess I'm just preoccupied. You know."

Scott's face fell, and he averted his eyes.

Seeing Scott hurt made Elizabeth feel awful. Nonetheless, she knew she had to work out this business with Tom one way or another. *And Scott and I will have all the time in the world to get to know each other in Denver,* Elizabeth reasoned as she smiled at him weakly. Right now she had more immediate things to take care of. Scott and skiing could wait.

"I think it's almost time for me to make my speech," she said brightly, unfolding a slip of paper in her pocket. "I scribbled this down just before the party—it's just a few sappy words of thanks to everyone, and then I'm going to toast Jessica."

"I bet Jessica will love that," Scott replied. "She sure does enjoy being the center of attention."

Elizabeth frowned at Scott's comment. It wasn't a very generous thing to say, even if it was true. But she decided to let it pass. Scott was probably just annoyed that Elizabeth was paying so much attention to everyone else.

"Where is Jessica anyway?" Elizabeth exclaimed,

her eyes continuing to rove over the crowd. She found Lila and Isabella, and she saw Nick talking to Steven, but Jessica was nowhere in sight. "I can't make the speech without her," she added.

Without her or *Tom,* she amended. Elizabeth hadn't quite figured out what to say yet, but she was planning to add something to her speech that, if Tom were listening, would act as an open invitation for him to speak to her later on. It would be a speech about good-byes and parting ways, but Elizabeth thought that perhaps she would also drop in some thoughts about memories . . . some hint about starting over. She would have to come up with something subtle, and yet it would have to stir Tom at the same time.

Although that won't work if he's not even here, she thought. She couldn't see Dana either, which was a bad sign. They were probably making out in some dark corner. *And here I am thinking about Tom, while I couldn't be further from his thoughts!*

Elizabeth sighed, feeling pressure mounting at her temples. A headache! Just what she needed. *I should just grab Jessica, make a speech, and then politely excuse myself when I can,* she thought, staring into her champagne glass. Perhaps it was the champagne, or else all the back-and-forthing she'd been doing over Tom and her decision to leave.

Champagne, Elizabeth thought in disgust, looking at her half-empty glass. *Why am I even drinking this stuff? I hate champagne. And I'm certainly not in the mood for celebrating.*

"I'll go find Jessica for you," Scott offered, a tentative smile on his face. "I think I saw her go into the kitchen."

"Thanks, Scott," Elizabeth replied, squeezing his shoulder. She felt another pinch of guilt as she watched him walk away. *He's been so patient with me,* she thought. *And that should count for something.* He'd been supportive and caring despite Elizabeth's mood swings. *Maybe I should be focusing on all of Scott's good qualities instead of on whether or not Tom still cares if I exist.* She rubbed the back of her neck, which had begun to ache. It was all so unfair: Scott cared for her, she still cared for Tom. And for all she knew, Tom didn't care if she lived or died.

"I think it's time the chef put down her wooden spoon," Winston declared, putting his arms around Denise's waist as she stood over the stove. "Take off the apron," he began, untying the bow at Denise's back, "let down your hair . . . in every sense," he continued, unpinning Denise's tight bun, "and come and party with Sweet Valley's most popular man."

Denise giggled. "And who might that be?"

"The one, the only, the smoldering hunk that has everyone talking . . . Winston Egbert, otherwise known as Beefy Bert."

"Beefy Bert?" Denise guffawed. "Can't you do

better than that, Winnie?" She turned around and put her arms around his neck.

"Uh . . . Wildman Win?"

"OK, OK, you tried," Denise replied. "Maybe you're right." She put down the spatula. "Maybe it's time to relax a little. We've been breaking our backs here."

"We sure have." Winston began nuzzling Denise's neck. "Everyone else is having a ball, and you and I are slaving away like second-class citizens."

Denise took off her apron, washed her hands, and smoothed her dress down over her hips. It was time for a little fun, and a few wild spins with Winston on the dance floor would be good for her back, which felt stiff after all the hours spent hunched over the chopping board. She stretched up her arms and flopped into a chair, taking out a compact to check her makeup.

"You look exquisite, doll face, so don't worry," said Winston, pulling at her hand. "Come ooonnn, I'm sick of being in this kitchen. I feel like we live here now."

"Just give me one second," Denise begged, applying a fresh coat of lipstick. "Let's just catch our breath for a moment before we brave the madhouse out there." She smiled and tilted her head up for a kiss.

"Mmm, you're right," Winston murmured as his lips touched Denise's. "There are some definite advantages to being stuck in the kitchen with you."

"You've got that right . . . Beefy Bert!" Denise chuckled and stroked Winston's cheek. "OK," she added, standing, "let's go and tango."

"Do you know how to tango?" Winston asked as he grabbed her hand and led her out of the kitchen.

"No, but I know how to salsa."

"Who doesn't?" Winston teased. "Maybe if you're lucky, I'll teach you how to tango."

"Right," Denise scoffed as they threaded their way through the clumps of people leaning against the passage walls, "like you're Mr. Coordination, Win."

"Just call me Fred Astaire!"

As they moved through the passage Denise spotted several people munching happily on her snacks, and she smiled with pride. She also noted that there were a lot of empty trays and bowls as they moved into the Theta living room, adding to her feeling of satisfaction. Despite the lobster debacle Denise knew she'd pulled off a big job *and* done it extremely well. There was no doubt in her mind that she would end up profiting from this down the road.

And you're going to need it, she reminded herself, her heart sinking momentarily as she thought of the huge debt she still had to pay off, the hole in her pocket that she'd been trying so hard to forget about. She shivered, recalling the cold, insistent voice of the debt collector. *I just have to hang in there a little longer,* Denise told herself as Winston pulled her through the crowd. *Soon my debts will be settled, and it will all seem like a distant bad dream. One day I may even laugh about this when I'm heading my own, extremely lucrative catering company!*

"Winston! Denise!" Bruce lumbered toward them, a glass of champagne in hand. "Lila and I were just talking about you. Grab some champagne and sit awhile." He pointed to a big comfy couch, and Denise sank onto it gratefully, smiling at Lila, who sat perched on one corner.

"Not a bad idea, Bruce," Denise replied. "Win, get us some bubbly. Let's recharge before we hit the dance floor. It's packed out there," she added, glancing through the doorway at the dance floor lit by the flashing strobe. "I'm not sure I can handle it yet."

"Well, one thing you *can* handle is catering," Lila praised with a warm smile. "You certainly have outdone yourself tonight, Denise. I'm really impressed. I must say, your cooking went way beyond my expectations."

"What did you expect? Tortilla chips and Cheez Whiz?" Denise asked, laughing.

"Not exactly," Lila replied. "But I didn't think the food would be so . . . sophisticated. I didn't think you'd know much about haute cuisine. Of course, I was sure the snacks would be tasty, but in a more . . . homey, working-class kind of way."

"I guess I should take that as a compliment," Denise said before taking a large gulp from the glass of champagne Winston handed her. "Oh, this is good stuff. It's going down like water."

"Well, it's not Dom Pérignon, but it will do." Lila arched an eyebrow and drained the rest of her glass.

"We're only students, remember, Li?" Winston said, waggling his finger. "This isn't one of your parents' parties."

"No, but speaking of which . . ." Lila shifted forward in her seat, her eyes flashing with excitement. "We have a great idea that I think you guys are going to like very much. Bruce, why don't you tell them."

"My parents are having a party tomorrow night," Bruce began, "and they had wanted it to be expensively catered, of course."

"Go on." Denise was getting excited. Perhaps what she'd been hoping for was already about to happen.

"The thing is, my mother's bored with all the usual fare. Sweet Valley is such a small place when it comes to this kind of stuff."

"When you're at a certain income level," Lila chimed in, "there are really only two or three catering options in Sweet Valley, and that gets dull after a while."

"Sure does," Bruce agreed. "So anyway, my folks had originally enlisted one of those two or three catering options to handle tomorrow night's party, but it appears they double booked themselves. They had planned on keeping *our* engagement, but my father *insisted* that the mayoral benefit for the Coalition to End World Hunger was much more important than our little soiree."

"That was big of him," Winston whispered.

Denise jabbed her boyfriend sharply in the ribs and pasted a bright smile on her face. "I see," she began. "So . . . you're in the market for a caterer?"

"Exactly!" Bruce cried as if he were amazed at Denise's powers of deduction. "And you know, Li and I think you and old Winston there would really fit the bill. Well, what do you say? Is that a great idea or what?"

"We would *love* to," Denise breathed. *This is like a dream come true!* she thought, awestruck. *Bruce's parents are beyond loaded. Not only will my financial troubles be sorted out, but it will be fun too!*

She turned to Winston excitedly. "Isn't that a cool idea?"

"Definitely," Winston replied, squeezing Denise's shoulder. "And, of course, I will be your adoring busboy, vegetable chopping boy, waiter, and general kitchen slave."

"My parents will pay you very well. That goes without saying," Bruce added. "Just make sure the food is as excellent as it was tonight."

"Naturally!" Denise exclaimed. "Don't worry,

Bruce, we'll go all out. Your parents will *not* be disappointed."

"Well," Bruce replied, "I love everything you made this evening, but it was the lobster *al* Denise that sealed it for me. Once I tried that, I knew my parents would be blown away. So be sure to have plenty of it on the menu."

At that, all the excitement and happiness Denise had been feeling disappeared in an instant, and in its place she felt a cold, dead weight like a heavy stone in the pit of her stomach. She caught Winston's eye and knew he was feeling the same.

If I use lobster, Denise thought miserably, *Bruce will be on to me in a second.* He would know it wasn't the same lobster *al* Denise he consumed in such vast quantities this evening. *But if I use tofu, there's no way Bruce's cultured parents and their oh-so-fancy guests will believe it's lobster.* After all, they weren't college kids. They'd know their lobster from their tofu!

"Uh," Denise began weakly, "don't you think it would be nicer to serve something else? I have all sorts of great ideas—and you know, lobster *al* Denise really isn't that fancy."

"Fancier than lobster?" said Lila. "Don't be ridiculous, Denise; it's the food of the gods."

"Besides," said Bruce, "you do it like no one else I know. No, you *have* to put it on the menu. No doubt about it."

Denise nodded glumly. *Maybe I should just say*

no, she said to herself. But on the other hand, she really needed the money, and just one job for Bruce's wealthy parents would more than likely clear her debt altogether. But how to fool Bruce and please his parents or fool his parents and please Bruce . . . that was the question. Was there a way out? Denise couldn't see one, but she knew she had no option but to try. "OK, Bruce," she said, "consider it a deal."

Something will come to me, Denise counseled herself. *By this time tomorrow I'll have an airtight plan. I'd better, or else I'm dead meat!*

Bored, Dana picked at an egg roll and watched as couples passed by her. Everyone seemed to be having a good time. Everyone but her.

The evening had started off well enough, with Tom picking her up and complimenting her on her hair. She'd spent all afternoon highlighting it, and she had to admit, it did come out looking stunning, the red-gold wisps framing her face perfectly. Still, most men never noticed these things, and it had come as a nice surprise to her when Tom had. He'd seemed very relaxed too and was attentive to her on the way to the party. They'd joked around, and things between them had seemed mellow and easy. Easier than Dana had thought they'd be. After all, they were going to Elizabeth Wakefield's party, and she knew that there was potential for Tom to freak out or, worse, just become silent and unreachable.

But he hadn't been that way at all. In fact, he'd been the picture of the adoring boyfriend. Once they'd arrived, he'd even insisted on getting her drinks, putting his arm around her, and introducing her to people she didn't know. Everything had been going as smoothly as could be. Until they'd hit the dance floor.

Dana's face darkened as she recalled the way Tom froze when he saw Elizabeth dancing with Scott. Up until then Tom had seemed more than content with Dana, holding her close, whispering flirtatious things in her ear and acting the way any guy who was interested in a girl would act. But then in a nanosecond it had all changed. Tom froze up like a Popsicle, and Dana's heart sank like a ten-ton brick. She didn't even have to follow the direction of Tom's eyes; she knew exactly what the cause was—or rather *who* it was.

Elizabeth Wakefield. Surprise, surprise.

Apart from her anger and hurt feelings for always coming in second to Elizabeth, Dana also felt *bored* by it. Simply bored and tired of the whole stupid thing. It was like a stuck record going around and around, over and over—*Tom sees Elizabeth, Tom gets upset, Dana tries to win him over and barely makes it by the skin of her teeth,* Dana mused. *How long will this go on? How much more energy do I have for this?*

However, in her heart of hearts, despite feeling as if she were at the end of her rope, Dana knew she would keep on fighting for Tom. She'd fight fair, but she'd fight dirty too. Whatever it took. She was hooked, and she knew it. Perhaps it was the thrill of never really being sure of her footing with Tom that kept her after him.

Dana considered this possibility. It might be true—all the guys who'd worshiped her, she'd immediately lost interest in. Or perhaps it was simply Tom's incredible body and brains and the way she felt when he kissed her—the level of chemistry between them. Dana didn't know, and she didn't care why she felt the way she did about Tom. All she knew was for whatever reason, she was crazy about him and didn't want to be with anyone else.

But it was becoming more and more difficult to hang on to Tom, especially now during Elizabeth's "last lap," as Dana called it, when everyone, including Tom, was paying her extra-special attention.

Dana polished off her egg roll and reached for another, deep in thought. *Maybe I shouldn't be so hard on Tom,* she mused. *He only danced with her once, and he probably just did it to be polite.* But deep down, Dana knew she was fooling herself.

Well, she thought, lifting her chin and flicking a crumb from her dress, *I don't care! I don't care if it is Elizabeth he really wants. If I'm around, it's just not going to happen. If it ever does, it'll be over my dead body!*

Caught up in her thoughts, Dana hadn't realized

she was staring into space until a blond head bobbed into her vision.

"Hey there, Dana." Scott Sinclair brushed past her and gave her a cryptic smile. "Have you seen your boyfriend lately?"

What is with *this guy?* Dana thought. He was so weird, he was almost creepy. "What's it to you?" Dana retorted, flashing Scott a cold look.

"What's it to *you* is more like it," Scott replied.

I give up, Dana thought as she studied Scott. Sure, the guy was good-looking and all, but considering that Elizabeth had once dated a fabulously perfect guy like Tom Watts, her taste sure had gone off. Still, Dana couldn't help being intrigued by Scott's question, and she recalled their last, equally peculiar conversation from a few days back.

Does he know something I don't? she wondered, heaving a sigh of impatience. "OK, Scott. No. No, I don't know where Tom is. He wandered off about fifteen minutes ago, and I haven't seen him since. Do *you* know where he is?"

Scott tilted his head in the direction of the kitchen, smiled slowly, and walked off without another word. Dana shook her head. This guy was a piece of work. But she couldn't resist heading for the kitchen. Perhaps there was something behind this after all.

Dana pushed through the swing door of the kitchen and entered, finding it empty. Something made her move to the window, though, and what she saw made her tremble in shock. Outside, beside a tree, stood Tom and Elizabeth, kissing passionately. At first Dana didn't want to believe her eyes, but it was a clear, moonlit night, and she knew her own boyfriend when she saw him. And as for Elizabeth, well, it was obviously her. Her blond hair was as bright as a lighthouse in the darkness.

Tears stung Dana's eyes as she looked on in horror, unable to tear herself away from the awful spectacle beyond the window. *What is the deal with Scott?* she thought, her despair and humiliation cutting through all the other wild emotions swirling around her. *Elizabeth is his girlfriend, and I'm with Tom. Why would he want me to see this?*

Chapter
Thirteen

*You're a real magnet tonight, Elizabeth Wakefield!
Everyone's deserted you—and you're the guest of
honor!*

Elizabeth drummed her fingers on the side of
her champagne glass impatiently. Where *was*
everyone? First Tom disappeared, then Jessica, and
then Scott went off to find Jessica and still hadn't
returned after almost ten minutes. If she was
going to make a speech, then it would have to be
soon. It was getting late.

As if in answer to her call, Elizabeth turned to
find Scott suddenly at her side. "Where have you
be—" She stopped herself, caught by the look on
Scott's face. His eyes were steely and glinting but
impenetrable, and his mouth was in a tight line.

"Elizabeth, I know you still have mixed feelings," he began, "so there's something I think you
should see." With that and without waiting for her

221

reply, Scott gripped Elizabeth's arm and led her to the kitchen, his movements brisk and jerky.

"Scott—" Elizabeth began, but she knew it was useless to continue protesting. He continued striding purposefully, his face a mask, his grip tight and imploring.

Scott pulled Elizabeth into the empty kitchen and pushed her toward the window. "There," he said. "This is the guy you've been losing sleep over. See for yourself who he really is."

Elizabeth felt a sudden, white-hot tremor spread up through her spine as she looked through the glass. What she saw, she could not believe.

Tom and . . . *Jessica!* Kissing in the garden. For a second everything slowed down, and Elizabeth felt the blood beating loudly in her eardrums.

No, she thought in disbelief, stumbling back from the window, her head reeling. She felt as if a roller coaster were screaming through her insides, and she laid her head against the cool wall, fighting for breath. *There has to be some mistake!*

Forcing her eyes back to the scene, Elizabeth blinked and looked again. There was no room for error. A bright shaft of moonlight illuminated the two of them—Tom and Jessica, kissing passionately. They were locked in a tight embrace, oblivious to everything around them. *But . . .* Elizabeth's thoughts rushed to her mind all at once and in a panic of confusion. *Tom wouldn't, couldn't . . . and Jessica?*

Her face blazing with anger and humiliation, Elizabeth turned slowly from the window, feeling a hot twist in her insides as if her stomach were being roasted on a spit. Then she bolted as fast as she could from the scene, pushing through the kitchen doors and running blindly past people, tears streaking down her cheeks. She didn't care if anyone saw her. She didn't care about anything.

There was nothing left to care about.

Stunned, Dana exhaled and slowly moved from the dark, cramped corner of the kitchen where she'd been hiding. What she'd just seen had thrown her into confusion. *If that was the real Elizabeth,* she thought, *then who . . . ? What . . . ?*

All of a sudden it became crystal clear. The whole scene swam into focus as if she'd just emerged from being deep underwater and opened her eyes to the world, sharp and solid around her. "Bingo!" she whispered to herself, and let out a low whistle.

That Scott sure was a schemer, but what Dana hadn't picked up before was that he was *on her side*. It was obvious. Together with Jessica, Scott had concocted a little scheme to keep Elizabeth and Tom apart. *Of course.* It was in his best interests to do so. They were all in the same boat, weren't they?

Dana thanked her lucky stars that she'd just seen what she'd seen. And it was all a question of fortunate timing. She'd heard Scott's voice as he entered the kitchen, and, acting quickly, Dana had slipped into a dark corner to spy on him. What a payoff! Seeing Scott's scheme and watching Elizabeth erupt into tears was a sweet sight for sore eyes.

Calmly Dana left the kitchen and made for the living room, no longer upset over Tom or Elizabeth or *anybody*—including herself. Everything was under control. Now sparks would fly between Tom and Elizabeth, but they wouldn't be the kind Tom had hoped for. And that would spell the end of Tom and Elizabeth for good, making way for the beginning of a long, happy era of Tom and Dana.

You see, Dana said to herself with a smile, *if you keep your eyes on the prize, it's yours in the end.*

Coolly Dana fixed herself a drink, keeping an eye out for Scott. She was awfully impressed. In her time Dana had come up with some pretty intricate scams, but this one took the cake. That Scott had faith in his abilities, even at the final hour. *He knows it's not over till it's over,* Dana thought. And no doubt he would have yet another plan lined up in the unlikely event that this one should fail. *I* must *have a little chat with him,* Dana noted. *I have to hear about his next move . . . and find out how I can get in on it.*

"Oh, Elizabeth," Tom murmured thickly, stroking her soft hair and pressing his cheek to hers. "It feels so good to hold you after all this time . . . after all we've been through." Again he sought out her lips with his own and kissed her deeply, every fiber of his being registering the love he felt in his heart. He closed his eyes again, savoring the feel of Elizabeth's mouth on his, the texture of the soft, pale skin at her neck, the scent of her perfumed hair.

Still, a part of him denied what he was experiencing. It was almost too good to bear believing in. *You could be dreaming, Watts,* Tom reminded himself. In that case he would simply keep his eyes shut tight to prolong the dream for as long as possible.

But Tom discovered there was no need to do that when he opened his eyes warily, testing himself for the second time. She was still there. It was still real. If only for this moment, Elizabeth was with him, and she was his.

This is the time, Tom thought as he gazed into Elizabeth's bright turquoise eyes. *This is the moment to say it, to tell the truth. No more lies. No more holding back. It's now or never.* For a minute Tom cast his mind back to all the history he and Elizabeth had had together—a history of friendship first, then love, then bitter, hostile resentment. They had felt it all, and finally they'd come full circle. Tom prayed that this time there would be no more obstacles to overcome, no more misunderstandings, no more arguments. He wanted to return to the way it had been in the beginning, when their love had been new and exciting and wonderful. They had been inseparable back then, sharing their every thought and feeling. It was time to have that again.

We deserve it, Tom realized. *And no matter what, even if Elizabeth still decides to go to Colorado, I will fight to keep this love.*

Looking at Elizabeth's sweet face, Tom knew he had to make his feelings clear. He had to lay his cards on the table and let her know how much she meant to him in case she had any doubts left. Tom took Elizabeth's small hands in his own and brought them to his lips. Already missing the warmth of her face so close to his, he impatiently rained kisses on her forehead, her eyelids, her temples, as if to make up for lost time. "I love you, Elizabeth Wakefield," he murmured against her soft cheek. "I have never stopped loving you."

"I love you too, Tom," Elizabeth whispered, sealing her declaration with a kiss so passionate and full of love that Tom felt as if he'd died and gone to heaven. *And if this is what it feels like,* he thought happily, *then I'm ready to go. . . .*

After she'd cried for a solid five minutes in a dark corner, something snapped in Elizabeth and she grew calm, went to the bathroom, splashed water on her face, and returned to the party. She didn't think anyone had seen her break down, and she was glad. She didn't want Tom or Jessica to have that satisfaction. She would be strong—at least on the surface.

Robotically Elizabeth switched off the music and clinked her glass with a fork, silencing everyone on the dance floor. With eyes as cold and hard as sapphires, Elizabeth surveyed the crowd in front of her while inside she felt anything but resilient. She felt as if every single little part of her had been mashed into a pulp—every truth she'd ever known, every emotion she'd ever believed in was reduced to nothing. *Just get through the next ten minutes,* she ordered herself. *You cannot break down in front of everyone.*

Fixing her eyes on a spot on the wall behind the crowd, Elizabeth cleared her throat and began to speak. Her voice sounded to her like it was coming from far away and belonged to someone else, but she pressed on, grateful that somewhere inside her she still had an autopilot who could help her through this terrible moment.

"It's wonderful to see so many familiar faces, and I feel very touched that you all came. Although I'm leaving Sweet Valley soon, I will never forget all of you who have contributed to my life here and made me feel so special."

Suddenly Elizabeth's voice faltered, and her eyes flickered down to see sympathetic looks on her friends' faces. For an instant a wild thought occurred to her. *They all know! They know about*

Tom and Jessica, and they feel sorry for me! But then just as quickly Elizabeth's rational side came to the rescue. *Nobody knows,* she told herself. *Except you and Scott.*

Elizabeth's gaze fell on Scott, and she saw in his face that he felt her pain. *I'm here,* his eyes seemed to say.

Clearing her throat again, Elizabeth willed her voice to stop shaking. She just had to go through the motions for one more minute, and then she could get out of there and deal with her sorrow in private. "I would like to thank my family," *and I will not bring myself to say the name Jessica even though these people expect me to,* "but most of all I'd like to thank Scott Sinclair for opening my eyes to the truth"—her voice wavered, breaking on the word *truth,* but she recovered—"and for helping me see the future."

As everyone applauded, Elizabeth stepped back, her face stony. Slowly she moved past everyone, thanking people and politely excusing herself. "It's all been too overwhelming," she said to Todd and Alex when they asked her why she was leaving. "I think I need to be alone now."

Elizabeth moved woodenly past Lila and Denise, a forced puppet's smile on her face, her eyes fixed on the door. Inside, her thoughts were a seething, jumbled mass.

For a moment the door was blocked by a group of smiling faces, and Elizabeth felt panic, hard and metallic, on the roof of her mouth. Then the group passed, and Elizabeth felt relief slide over her as the front door of Theta house swam into focus, as welcoming as light at the end of a dark and endless tunnel.

Almost there! she told herself, willing herself to be calm. But a pile of angry questions and conflicting emotions seethed and frothed in her head, causing her heart to race wildly. The door before her suddenly began to blur and swim in a sea of tears.

Why couldn't I have remained blind to what was happening in the garden? she wondered grimly. *I only have twenty-twenty vision when something can hurt me the most and hit me the hardest.*

"Hey, Elizabeth!"

Elizabeth turned her head slightly to see Isabella Ricci running after her. "Leaving so soon?" Isabella asked, her face falling when she'd obviously caught a glimpse of the tears glittering in Elizabeth's eyes.

Waving Isabella off, Elizabeth reached the door and flung it open, stumbling down the stairs and into the darkness. Now she couldn't hold back any longer. Hot, stabbing tears of anger started streaming down her cheeks, and she began to run, slowly at first, then breaking into a fast sprint as she made for the sanctuary of her dorm, the wind whipping her hair.

I'm gone, she said to herself. *Before I know it,*

I'll be gone. Away from Sweet Valley and all the awful memories it holds. Away from Jessica and Tom, the two people I loved most—and who betrayed me the hardest.

She felt numb, as if she'd been buried under ten feet of snow for a year. She couldn't feel anything anymore. All she could do was put one foot in front of the other and keep her eyes fixed on the path ahead of her. Now she had no more doubts. Her decision was made, and it was as irrevocable as a death sentence. As final as a shattered heart.

Elizabeth Wakefield is taking off on the next plane to Denver! Can Tom Watts and Jessica Wakefield find a way to keep her in Sweet Valley? Or have they gone too far already? Find out in Sweet Valley University #38, GOOD-BYE, ELIZABETH.

SIGN UP FOR THE SWEET VALLEY HIGH® FAN CLUB!

Hey, girls! Get all the gossip on Sweet Valley High's® most popular teenagers when you join our fantastic Fan Club! As a member, you'll get all of this really cool stuff:

- Membership Card with your own personal Fan Club ID number
- A Sweet Valley High® Secret Treasure Box
- Sweet Valley High® Stationery
- Official Fan Club Pencil (for secret note writing!)
- Three Bookmarks
- A "Members Only" Door Hanger
- Two Skeins of J. & P. Coats® Embroidery Floss with flower barrette instruction leaflet
- Two editions of *The Oracle* newsletter
- Plus exclusive Sweet Valley High® product offers, special savings, contests, and much more!

Be the first to find out what Jessica & Elizabeth Wakefield are up to by joining the Sweet Valley High® Fan Club for the one-year membership fee of only $6.25 each for U.S. residents, $8.25 for Canadian residents (U.S. currency). Includes shipping & handling.

Send a check or money order (do not send cash) made payable to "Sweet Valley High® Fan Club" along with this form to:

SWEET VALLEY HIGH® FAN CLUB, BOX 3919-B, SCHAUMBURG, IL 60168-3919

NAME_____
(Please print clearly)

ADDRESS_____

CITY_____ STATE _____ ZIP_____
(Required)

AGE _____ BIRTHDAY_____ / _____ / _____

Offer good while supplies last. Allow 6-8 weeks after check clearance for delivery. Addresses without ZIP codes cannot be honored. Offer good in USA & Canada only. Void where prohibited by law.
©1993 by Francine Pascal   LCI-1383-193

BFYR 135